Dead End . . .

Maggie turned a corner and slammed into a wall. Her hand touched something wet and slimy.

And then she heard a dry fluttering overhead, like hundreds of tiny umbrellas opening all at once.

Something brushed her face. Something furry. She screamed!

"Help me! Somebody—help me! Get me out of here!"

The tunnel vibrated with the sound of a thousand flapping wings.

The footsteps crunched closer.

Screaming for help. Maggie ran into another cold, wet wall.

I'm trapped, she realized.

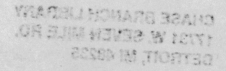

Bad Dreams

Simon Pulse
New York London Toronto Sydney

A Parachute Press Book

SIMON PULSE
An imprint of Simon & Schuster Children's Publishing Division
1230 Avenue of the Americas, New York, NY 10020
Copyright © 1994 by Parachute Publishing, L.L.C.

SIMON PULSE and colophon are registered trademarks of
Simon & Schuster, Inc.
FEAR STREET is a registered trademark of Parachute Press, Inc.
Manufactured in the United States of America
First Archway Paperback edition March 1994
First Simon Pulse edition June 2005
20 19 18 17 16 15 14

ISBN-13: 978-0-671-78569-7
ISBN-10: 0-671-78569-9

Bad Dreams

prologue

"**N**o . . . no . . ."

The girl tossed fitfully in the large canopy bed, mumbling in her sleep. "Please—no—stay away."

If only she could wake up. If only she could open her eyes, then she'd be safe. Safe in her bed, safe in her house on Fear Street.

But she couldn't wake up.

"No . . . no . . ." Her moans grew louder.

"NOOO!"

Suddenly, the girl sat straight up in bed, wide awake. She shuddered, gasping for breath. Grabbing the covers, she glanced around her dark, familiar bedroom.

No one here. Just a bad dream.

Just a bad dream. She repeated the words over and over like a lullaby.

From her bed, she could see out the window. She peered out at another cold fall night. The large old

1

maple shivered in the icy breeze, dropping its last leaves. Through the bare branches of the tree, she could see the streetlight, casting an eerie yellow glow.

She sank back against the pillows, wet with sweat. Her long blond hair was matted to her head.

I'd be better off not sleeping at all, she told herself. She sighed softly, feeling a little better now. She closed her eyes.

Which is when she felt the presence.

Felt that she *wasn't* alone in the room, after all.

Her eyes snapped back open. She had never been so alert in her whole life.

What made her so sure there was someone there? She didn't know.

"Who is it?" she whispered.

No answer. She sat up slowly, clutching the bedsheet to her. She stared into the room's dark corners, studied the shadows.

Then she saw it.

A glint of light in the far corner.

She opened her mouth to speak but was too frightened. For she was now able to make out the human figure who lurked in the corner of her room.

She heard an angry growl.

Then the darkness exploded. The other girl rushed out at her so quickly, she didn't have time to react.

The knife came down.

The first blow missed. She struggled desperately, trying to twist away.

But she was tangled in the covers now, and the girl was holding her down.

2

"Sister—!" she protested, trying to push her away. *"But you're my sister!"*

She tried to scream but hadn't enough breath.

She forced herself up, but her attacker shoved her back, smashing her skull hard against the headboard.

For a moment everything went black.

Then she felt a searing stab of pain.

And again.

And again.

And then darkness closed in on her from all sides.

In the eerily silent room, nothing moved now except for the trembling canopy over the bed.

chapter

1

Maggie Travers's bad dreams didn't start until the night she slept in the canopy bed for the first time.

The bed was just one of the surprises awaiting Maggie and her family at their new house on Fear Street.

But for a while, it appeared the Travers family would never *find* the house.

Maggie had stared at the map in her lap, trying to trace the route to Fear Street with her finger. She pushed a strand of long red hair behind one ear. It fell right back again. "I guess we turn left here," she told her mother.

Mrs. Travers slowed the car to a crawl. She peered through the windshield into the glare of the sunny spring afternoon. "Are you sure?"

"No, she's *not* sure," Andrea grumbled from the

backseat. "I told you, Mom—we should have turned right on Canyon Road. But, nooo, Maggie says go straight, so you go straight. It's so stupid!"

Maggie kept quiet. She didn't want to start a fight with her sister. Starting a fight with Andrea was one of the easiest things in the world. *Not* starting a fight with Andrea—now *that* was tricky.

Gus, Maggie's old golden retriever, was sharing the backseat with Andrea. The dog had his head out the window. He gave a low, pitiful growl.

Maggie glanced in her side mirror. Gus was wearing the forlorn look he always had on during car trips. I know how you feel, Maggie told him silently.

It was Saturday. The day of their big move had finally arrived. We're off to a terrific start, Maggie thought grimly.

They were supposed to follow the huge white whale of a moving van. But then Andrea had insisted on stopping at a 7-Eleven for Cokes. They had lost the van, Maggie misread the map, and now they were wandering through a maze of streets that circled north of town toward the Fear Street woods for almost—

Maggie glanced at her watch. Ten after three! She would never get to practice now! The other girls on the Shadyside High swim team must be wondering where they were.

"We're missing practice," she informed her sister.

Andrea rolled her eyes. "Naturally," she muttered unhappily.

"If only we could find someone out walking,"

Mrs. Travers said, nervously brushing her reddish gray hair back with her hand. "We could ask where we are."

"We're lost," Andrea said. "That's where we are. Thanks to you-know-who."

"We were supposed to be following the moving van," Maggie reminded her sister as calmly as she could.

"What does that have to do with anything?" Andrea shot back.

Maggie sighed. It seemed as if Andrea wanted to argue no matter what. "Look," Maggie said, "I'm just saying it's not all my fault, okay?"

"Who said to go straight?" Andrea demanded. "Gus?"

Maggie tried to keep her face blank, but she could feel her anger mounting. It always worked this way. No matter how many times she told herself not to let Andrea get her angry, she got angry.

Maggie tried to push the large, unwieldy street map back to her sister. "You want to take over?" she asked. "Here. If you think you can do better, be my guest."

"No thanks," Andrea muttered. "I'm sure I couldn't do it as well as you. You do *everything* better."

"Well—" Maggie began.

Mrs. Travers gave her older daughter a warning glance. "Maggie," she said. "Please."

Maggie felt her face flush. It seemed as if Mrs. Travers was always warning her to go easy on

Andrea. Always explaining how Andrea had it much harder than Maggie did.

Maggie was seventeen, Andrea sixteen. But the way their mom acted, you'd think Andrea was five.

Maggie glanced back at her sister, who was now staring out the window, scowling, her jaw jutting forward in that way she had when she was frustrated. Maggie felt her anger easing, a rush of pity taking its place. Mom was right. She *should* go easy on Andrea.

With their red hair and green eyes, she and Andrea looked a lot alike. But the same features that made Maggie pretty—the green eyes, the red hair, the high cheekbones—just didn't fit together right on Andrea.

Maggie was tall and thin; Andrea shorter with a broadness in her shoulders that bordered on stocky. Also, Maggie's long red hair was thick and wavy. Andrea's shoulder-length hair was fine and always hung limp and straight, no matter what she did.

Looks weren't Maggie's only advantage. Maggie had always been one step ahead of her sister in everything—grades, sports, guys.

There was no doubt about it, she thought sadly. This move was going to be harder on Andrea than any of them.

After all, Andrea had never been very popular at school, and the one thing she felt she had going for her was that she was a North Hills girl.

North Hills was the most exclusive section of Shadyside. Andrea liked the status of North Hills. She loved hanging out at the country club. Maggie winced when she remembered how Andrea and her friends had snubbed kids from other parts of town.

Well, now they were leaving North Hills far behind. And all the kids Andrea had snubbed over the years would have the last laugh.

I will not argue with my sister, Maggie told herself. I will not, I will not, she thought, as if her mind were a blackboard and some teacher had assigned her to write the words over and over.

Maggie still felt guilty. And the feeling came back every time she argued with Andrea.

She'd been arguing with Andrea the day their dad died.

So dumb. There wasn't any milk for cereal that morning.

Andrea blamed Maggie for finishing the milk the night before. Maggie protested that she hadn't touched the milk. Then Andrea called her a liar.

They were off in an angry torrent of words. Maggie found herself reminding Andrea of things that had happened years before. Like the time when Andrea was seven and she had set fire to the hair on Maggie's favorite Barbie doll.

Then Andrea started yelling that Maggie had ruined her life. She sputtered angry nonsense about how Maggie stole any guy she was interested in.

By then, they were shrieking at each other and Andrea was crying. And then Mr. Travers told Maggie to stop picking on her sister. That made Maggie so mad, she dumped her bowl of dry cereal on the floor.

It was one of the great injustices in Maggie's life. Andrea could have a tantrum, scream, cry, break plates, whatever. Everyone was used to her fits.

But let Maggie lose it one little bit, and her parents acted as if the whole house had blown up.

Right after she had dumped the cereal, Maggie felt ashamed.

Her dad's face turned bright red. "I am so fed up with this bickering!" he yelled. "Really, Maggie. Why can't you act your age?"

Then he scooted his chair back, tossed down his newspaper, and stormed out of the house.

That was the last time Maggie saw him.

Mr. Travers had a stroke that afternoon in his office while sitting at his desk. When his secretary found him, he was already dead.

I never even got a chance to apologize, Maggie thought bitterly.

They were still sitting at the intersection. "Well," Mrs. Travers said, sighing, "we should try *something.*" She turned left.

"Of *course* you listen to Maggie," Andrea griped.

Gus barked twice.

"That's right, Gus," Mrs. Travers said, "you tell them." To her daughters, she added, "Gus wants you two to stop bickering."

Despite the tension between them, Maggie and Andrea shared a quick grin. Their mother's belief in the knowledge and wisdom of animals was legendary in the Travers family.

The Traverses' mailbox was always stuffed with

mailings from all the animal rights groups Mrs. Travers had once given money to. She was *always* telling them what Gus was thinking.

"I hope we're not getting close to our new house," Andrea murmured, staring out the window. "Please tell me this isn't where we're going to be living."

Andrea was right, Maggie thought. The house had looked pretty bad the day Mom drove them over to see it. But that day it had been pouring, and they figured it was the rain that made the house and the neighborhood so gloomy.

Somehow today's bright sunshine just made the neighborhood seem even drearier. All the houses needed to be painted. They were all so shabby, so run-down.

"Welcome to burglar city," Andrea joked, pretending to do a tour-guide voice. "Our neighborhood is proud to announce we have one of the highest crime rates in the country."

Maggie laughed, but she could feel her heart fluttering. The thought of burglars had always terrified her, even when they were living in North Hills, where break-ins were almost unheard of.

Mrs. Travers frowned. "I know this part of town isn't the greatest, girls," she said, "but it's all we can afford now." She forced a smile. "Anyway, we've got old Gus to protect us."

Right, thought Maggie. If a robber broke in, Gus would be all over him. But the only danger for the robber would be that Gus might lick him on the lips and gross him out!

"Look!" Maggie cried suddenly, pointing to the

green sign tilted into the intersection. "Fear Street! We found it! We're not lost after all!"

Mrs. Travers cheered. Maggie felt a surge of relief. Her good mood lasted until she saw the house.

Twenty-three Fear Street seemed even more ramshackle and neglected than it had the last time. Two of the green shutters were now hanging by single rusty hinges. The lawn had huge brown patches and looked dead. As did the whole place.

Maggie shivered.

The big white moving van was parked out front, and men were carrying furniture up the front walk. Maggie watched two burly men in green uniforms disappear through the front door, struggling with her dresser. She wanted to tell them to turn around, to bring everything back to North Hills. But this was home now.

Mrs. Travers turned in her seat to face her daughters. She was smiling, but under the smile Maggie saw worry. "Girls," she said, "I know it doesn't look like much, but when we have more money, we can paint it and fix it up and plant some flowers and it really will look quite nice. You wait and see. Besides, fixing it up will be fun."

Maggie forced a smile. The move was hard on her mom too, she knew. "Well," Maggie said, clapping her hands together, "let's get started."

She climbed out of the car and stretched. Gus was thumping his tail against the backseat, watching her every move. "Just a second, Gus," she told him.

Mrs. Travers waved to the moving men. "We got a little lost," she called.

The workers didn't even nod back. "Mom," Maggie said, tugging on her arm, "I need the trunk key."

They had brought their valuables and clothes in the car. Maggie inserted the key into the lock, popped open the trunk, and started unloading suitcases. She pulled out her green bag and carefully set it down on the sidewalk.

Gus was barking like crazy. Andrea leaned against the car, staring into space. "Andrea, you going to give us a hand here?" Mrs. Travers asked sharply.

Making a face, Andrea walked over and selected the smallest—and lightest—bag. She instantly thumped it back down on the sidewalk. "Oh, poor Gus," she said, opening the car door. "You must be dying of the heat in there."

"Wait, Andrea, not yet," Maggie warned.

Too late.

Gus burst out of the car. He started running in circles around Andrea's legs. Then he raced over to Mrs. Travers, jumping up on her, then over to Maggie.

"Easy, Gus," Maggie told him. The next thing she knew, Gus was running off down the block. Maggie had her hands full of suitcases. "Gus!" she yelled.

The dumb dog didn't stop.

"Quick, Andrea. Go get him!" cried Mrs. Travers.

"It's *Maggie's* dog," replied Andrea peevishly. "Let *Maggie* get him."

Maggie started to point out that Andrea was the one who had let Gus out. But she saw the annoyance on her mother's face. *"I'll* get him," she said, sighing.

She dropped the suitcases and started to run after Gus. He was down at the end of the block, "decorating" somebody's hedge. "Gus!" she yelled again.

He didn't even pick his head up to listen. He trotted on.

She ran faster.

She was running flat out, her sneakers smacking the pavement hard.

Gus had turned the corner, out of sight. "Gus!" she yelled again.

Then she reached the corner. And slid to a halt.

Gus was ambling across a lawn on the other side of the street. But when he saw Maggie, he started running straight toward her.

He took the shortest route.

Right through the middle of the street.

Right into the path of a speeding delivery truck.

"Gus—*stop!"* Maggie shrieked.

She shut her eyes and heard the dog's shrill yelp of pain.

chapter
2

*T*ires squealed. A horn blared. The truck skidded.

With the dog's pitiful yelp still in her ears, Maggie screamed.

Without realizing it, she had clamped her hands over her eyes. Trembling all over, she slowly removed them—and stared at Gus, standing shaken but unhurt, on the sidewalk.

The poor dog, she realized, must have yelped in fear—not pain.

The truck had stopped several yards ahead. The driver leaned out, his round face red with fury. "Get that stupid mutt on a leash!" he bellowed.

"Sorry," Maggie called. But when the truck took off, she let out a whoop of joy.

"Oh, Gus! You're okay! You're okay!" She fell to her knees, her arms thrown open wide. "Gus! Come here, boy!"

Gus came trotting over obediently. She threw her long arms around the dog's graying head and hugged him tightly. "Sure," she murmured, *"now* you're obedient."

Gus waited patiently until Maggie finally let him go. This time she kept a firm grip on his collar.

Panting with his mouth open, the dog looked as if he were smiling. Maggie kissed the top of Gus's head.

I couldn't bear another death in the family, she thought grimly. I just couldn't bear it.

Maggie led Gus back to the house and in through the front door. She bumped into a moving man coming the other way.

"Watch it!" he muttered rudely.

As soon as Maggie let Gus go free, the old dog took off, sniffing everywhere, exploring the new house. He ran into the living room, where Andrea was relaxing on the Travers's white-and-gray-striped sofa. The sofa looked lost in the empty room.

In the kitchen, Mrs. Travers was scrubbing away at the soot and dust and grime on the stovetop. Mrs. Travers could be spacey about a lot of things, but when it came to dirt, she was focused—a cleaning machine.

She waved a yellow-rubber-gloved hand at Maggie and Andrea. "Well," she said, "I think I've made some important archaeological discoveries in the kitchen. We've got about ten layers of dirt in here!"

Maggie gazed at her sister, whose features were

tight with unhappiness. "Andrea," she said gently, "why don't we start setting up our rooms? We'll probably feel better when we've got our own stuff in them."

"I doubt it," Andrea grumbled. But she trudged upstairs after Maggie.

"Now, don't get discouraged about how it looks," their mom called after them. "It just needs a little dusting. I'll be up there as soon as I finish in the kitchen."

It was going to take more than dusting to make this place livable, Maggie thought. The wallpaper in the hall was supposed to be white with a rose pattern. But the paper had yellowed and was peeling, and the roses looked as if they had died.

She turned right at the top of the stairs. Their bedrooms were at the end of the hall. She led the way and turned right into the room she had chosen while Andrea turned left into hers.

"Whoa!" Maggie uttered a low cry and stopped in the doorway.

There it stood.

A beautiful, old-fashioned four-poster canopy bed.

Dark, polished wood. And with a pink canopy on top.

"Oh, my goodness!" Maggie whispered. She blinked. As if to make sure the bed was real, she crossed the room and sat down on it.

"Unbelievable," she said softly. The previous owners had left the bed behind!

17

But why? Why did they leave the bed and nothing else?

What a mystery.

"You've got to be kidding!" Andrea exclaimed from the doorway. She had heard Maggie's delighted cries.

Maggie stood up and gestured to the bed, grinning. "Can you believe it?"

Andrea was circling the bed now, her mouth open. She ran her hands down the old wooden posts. "How could they leave this?"

Maggie shook her head. "I don't know. Maybe they didn't like it anymore."

Even as she said it, the explanation seemed silly. How could *anyone* not like this bed?

"It's so *gorgeous!*" Andrea gasped. "Look at the carving on the posts."

She was right. The woodwork was stunning, with intricate carved pinecones poking over the top of the canopy. "Do you think they're going to come back for it?" Andrea asked.

Maggie frowned. That hadn't occurred to her. Maybe she wouldn't get to keep the bed after all. "Beats me," she said thoughtfully. "Why would they take everything else and leave this for later? It doesn't make sense."

"You're right," Andrea said. "I think they deliberately left it behind."

Andrea gave Maggie a friendly smile. I know that smile, Maggie thought. In fact, Maggie could predict everything that was about to happen.

Andrea was trying to act calm, but Maggie could tell how tense she was. And she knew why Andrea was tense. Andrea wanted the bed. Desperately.

"Say, Mags," Andrea began. "Mags, you know how I've always wanted an old-fashioned bed like this one, right?" Andrea bit her lip.

Here came the question Maggie had silently predicted.

Sure enough, Andrea demanded, "Can I have it?"

Can I have it?—Andrea's four favorite words.

Andrea stared at Maggie, pleading with her eyes. Maggie lowered hers to the bed.

What should I tell her? Maggie asked herself. What should I do?

Should I avoid a fight and give it to her?

What should I say?

If Maggie had known the horrors that awaited her in the old canopy bed, her answer might have been different.

But she had no way of knowing why the bed had been left behind.

chapter
3

"*F*inders keepers," Maggie told her sister.

Andrea flinched as if Maggie had punched her. "Finders keepers? Oh, give me a break!" Andrea cried heatedly. "You're not going to be that childish, are you?"

Maggie's smile faded fast. "It's not childish. We chose the rooms last time we were here. You wanted the bigger room, the one in the back of the house, the quiet room, off the street. Remember? The one with the great window seat."

"But that was before we knew they were going to leave the bed behind," Andrea whined. "It's not fair."

"Andrea," Maggie said. "I'm sorry. It was just luck. Look, sometimes I get lucky, sometimes you—"

"That's such bull, Maggie, and you know it!" Andrea snapped. "You *always* get your way!"

"No, that's not true, that's—"

"It *is* true! I don't believe you! You never give me a break! Never! You are a totally selfish pig!"

As far as Maggie was concerned, it was always Andrea who started the name-calling and yelling first. It was certainly true now. Andrea was shrieking at the top of her lungs.

The louder Andrea yelled, the quieter Maggie became. "Andrea, what if the bed had been in *your* room? Would you give it up?"

Andrea had been pacing around the bed. Now she slapped her forehead in disbelief. *"I would if all your life you had dreamed of having a canopy bed!"* she screamed.

"All your life, since when, Andrea?" Maggie replied. She was trying to remain calm, but her voice was shaking. "Since five minutes ago?"

She could hear footsteps hurrying up the stairs.

"Mom!" Andrea pleaded as Mrs. Travers hurried into the bedroom. "You tell her! Haven't I always wanted a canopy bed? Haven't I?"

"Hold it, hold it, hold it," Mrs. Travers said wearily. "Please, whatever you do, don't shout." Then her eyes fell on the bed, and her jaw dropped.

"Oh, my goodness," Mrs. Travers cried. Her eyes lit up. "They left that beautiful antique behind?"

"Yes!" cried Andrea. "And Maggie says—"

Mrs. Travers wasn't listening. She walked across the room slowly and stared at the bed as if it were a mirage. "This must be worth over a thousand dollars," she said softly. "Why would they leave it behind? I hope there's nothing wrong with it. It's not rotted or infested or something . . ."

"It's perfect," Andrea insisted. "And Maggie claims that it's hers because it's in her room, which is so childish, I—"

She didn't get any further. Mrs. Travers held up a hand like a traffic cop. "Wait a second, Andrea. I don't want an argument about this. I mean, this is something to celebrate."

"I'm supposed to *celebrate* because Maggie got a great bed?" Andrea made a disgusted face.

"You're supposed to celebrate because we *all* got a great bed," Mrs. Travers told her. "But since Maggie picked this room, Maggie gets to sleep in it. What's the big deal?"

"But that's soooo unfair!" Andrea wailed.

Mrs. Travers rarely spoke sharply. Instead, her expression became pained, as if she was going to cry.

They had all done plenty of that in the seven months since Mr. Travers had died. But Mrs. Travers had cried more than any of them. Maggie and Andrea had both been awakened many nights by their mother's sobs. They would try to comfort her, but never could.

So when she got that about-to-cry tightness on her face, as she had now, it shut them both up. Andrea gritted her teeth, but didn't say another word.

"I can't believe you two," Mrs. Travers said, crossing her slender arms over the front of her sweatshirt. "The way you are always at each other's throats, people would think you hate each other."

But we do, Maggie thought bitterly. Even Daddy's death hasn't brought us closer together.

We *do* hate each other.

That night they planned on making dinner at home, but Mrs. Travers couldn't find the box with the kitchen stuff. So even though they were on a tight budget, she took her daughters out to a restaurant.

Maggie managed to make it through the meal without fighting with Andrea. That was the good news. The bad news was nobody said much of anything. Well, that wasn't too surprising, Maggie told herself. They were all exhausted.

"I just wish we could go back to our old house," Andrea grumbled as they were finishing dinner. "Even without any of our stuff there, it would still be better."

Mrs. Travers didn't answer. Neither did Maggie. What was there to say?

Maggie slung an arm around her sister's shoulders as they walked out of the restaurant. I'm going to keep this family close, she told herself. If it's the last thing I do.

When they returned to the house on Fear Street, Maggie got her first peek at the place in the dark. The house was run-down and ugly in bright sunshine. No surprise that it loomed dark and creepy at night.

The phone rang as they ran inside. "Our first call!" Andrea cried excitedly, racing for the phone.

Her face fell when she answered. "Just a sec," she said, sighing. She dropped the receiver so that it dangled down from the phone. "For you," she told Maggie as she walked away dejectedly. "Always for you," Maggie heard her mutter under her breath.

When Maggie picked up the phone, a familiar voice said brightly, "Hey, how's the new house?"

"Justin!" Maggie exclaimed. She had been going out with Justin Stiles for only a few weeks and still couldn't quite believe it. Justin had to be the most popular guy at Shadyside High.

One of Maggie's best friends on the swim team, Dawn Rodgers, had dated him the past year. When Justin first asked Maggie out, Dawn had warned Maggie that Justin had a "wandering eye."

But right then Maggie didn't care. She was just glad his eye had wandered in her direction!

Justin had sexy wavy brown hair and gorgeous ice-blue eyes that made Maggie melt.

"So what's up with the new house?" he asked.

"It's like something out of *The Addams Family*," Maggie told him dryly.

"It is not!" Maggie's mother called from the living room.

"It *is*," Maggie whispered. "It looks like one of those houses you see in horror movies, where green gunk starts to pour out of the walls."

Justin snickered. "Sounds like my kind of place!"

Maggie groaned.

They were both silent. She tried to think of something to say.

24

"So when can I see it?" Justin asked.

"Never," Maggie told him. "Seriously. I'm way too embarrassed. You can't come over here—ever."

Justin laughed, but this time it sounded a little tense. "So what are you trying to tell me?"

Maggie grinned. It delighted her to think that Justin might be feeling a little insecure about their relationship—even for a single second. Justin Stiles? Insecure? From everything she had heard about Justin, that would be a major switch.

"Let's see. How about coming over—uh, tomorrow afternoon?" she asked. So much for playing it cool.

"Awesome," he replied. "Later, Mags."

The moment she hung up, the phone rang again.

Andrea hurried in from the living room. It was for Maggie again.

"We missed you this afternoon," said a cheerful voice. "You ready to lose the hundred-meter tomorrow?"

"Hi, Dawn," Maggie said, leaning against the wall and shifting the phone to her other ear. Dawn Rodgers was the best swimmer on the team—after Maggie, of course. "As a matter of fact, I just could lose," said Maggie. "I haven't been in the pool all week!"

"Good," said Dawn. "Maybe I have a chance." Then she laughed.

So far this season Maggie had managed to edge Dawn out in every race. Dawn was the most competitive person Maggie had ever met, but she was a pretty good sport about coming in second.

25

"Anyway," Dawn said, "that's not why I called. You *know* why I called, don't you?"

Maggie smiled. "I just talked to Justin a second ago," she replied.

"You're a mind reader," Dawn said, giggling.

Maggie started telling Dawn about Justin's call. She leaned back against the wall, smiling dreamily. Being with Justin was the best. But talking about it with her friends afterward was a close second!

As she talked to Dawn, Maggie could see Andrea staring at her from the other room.

Why is she glaring at me like that? Maggie wondered.

Why does she have to stare at me and listen to my conversations?

Give me a break, Andrea. Get a life!

They went to bed at ten. They were all worn out from unpacking.

Maggie and Andrea shared a bathroom at the end of the hall. Saying she would be only a minute, Andrea insisted on going in first.

"Hey—get out!" Maggie finally complained twenty minutes later. She rapped hard on the bathroom door.

The door flew open, and a burst of steam hit Maggie in the face. Andrea's red hair was plastered to her skull, and she was glowering. "The water pressure stinks!" Andrea cried. "And I had to let the shower run for a year before the brown water stopped coming out! I don't think anyone's used these pipes since the Civil War!"

Maggie wanted to complain about Andrea hogging the bathroom, but she held back. She forced a smile. "Well, sleep well," she said.

"In this disgusting haunted house?" Andrea exclaimed. "Fat chance." She stomped into her room and closed the door.

The canopy bed was even prettier since Maggie had covered it with her pink sheets and the thin white afghan her grandmother had knit for her. She stopped to admire it for the hundredth time. It was awesome!

Maggie moved to the window. In the pale light from the moon, she could see tiny buds opening on the old maple tree that grew right up to her window. That seemed like a good sign. And Justin's call had made her happy. He was coming by tomorrow!

She yawned. She really was exhausted. She changed into a nightshirt, dropping her clothes on the one chair the movers had brought upstairs.

Maggie loved getting into a well-made bed. She felt so protected when she was tucked in tight.

She lay on her back and gazed up at the canopy overhead. More protection.

Maggie closed her eyes. She settled in, feeling her muscles start to relax.

Usually she had trouble falling asleep in a new bed. This time, she drifted to sleep before she knew it.

And then came the first dream.

In the beginning it was a pretty dream. She was floating. No. Falling. Falling slowly through a swirling pink haze.

Then the mist grew heavier, darker. The pink disappeared, replaced by ugly harsh grays.

Through the ugly mist, she saw a girl.

What was cold? What felt suddenly cold?

Had the dark mist turned cold? Or was it the girl?

She saw the girl's head, her long ash-blond hair. . . .

But she couldn't see the girl's face.

I want to see her face, Maggie dreamed.

Why can't I see her face? Is something wrong with it?

She knew she was dreaming. And she knew she was scared.

The dream wasn't pretty anymore.

Something was wrong. Something was wrong with the girl.

Why doesn't she move? Maggie wondered. Why can't I see her face?

The girl is in trouble, Maggie knew all at once.

The girl is in terrible trouble.

She tried to move closer, but the heavy mist pushed her back.

She tried to see the girl's face, but the mist deepened, the mist swirled over and around her like a heavy curtain, blanketing the girl from view.

And then Maggie heard a hideous scream.

chapter
4

*T*he scream rose shrilly, like someone's dying shout.

Maggie sat up, her heart pounding, her eyes wide open.

Who screamed? And why?

Breathing hard, she stared into the dark room. Was she alone?

Yes. But where was she?

This isn't my room, she thought.

This isn't my house.

Then she remembered. This was her new house, her new room.

She gasped as Andrea and her mom came running in. Sitting straight up in bed, gripping the white afghan to her chest, Maggie stared at them, dazed and frightened.

"Wh-what was that scream?" her mother demanded fearfully.

Maggie realized that it was *she* who had let out the long, bloodcurdling scream. "Bad dream," she murmured, more than a little embarrassed.

"Oh, thank goodness," her mom said, sitting down heavily on the bed. "The way you screamed, I thought . . ."

"A real nightmare, huh?" Andrea asked quietly, sitting at the foot of the bed and wrapping her hand around the carved bedpost.

Maggie's breathing slowly returned to normal. She forced a smile. It felt good to have them there.

"It—it seemed so real," she stammered.

"Well, dreams do quite often," Mrs. Travers said. She patted her daughter's shoulder. Maggie was starting to feel a little foolish, as if she were three years old.

"Tell it to us," Andrea suggested, "before you forget it."

"I don't think I'll ever forget it," Maggie told her. "It was just a girl sleeping. The way she was sleeping —at first I thought she was dead. Then she started twisting and turning. She looked—I don't know— tortured. I could feel she was in trouble."

"Weird," said Andrea. "What did she look like?"

"I couldn't see her face, but she had long blond hair."

"Dawn Rodgers," Andrea guessed. "You talked to Dawn tonight."

It was true. Dawn did have long blond hair. But the girl in the dream was an ash blond, with paler hair than Maggie had ever remembered seeing outside a magazine. "Maybe it was Dawn," she told Andrea. "I don't know."

Mrs. Travers brushed a lock of hair from Maggie's forehead. "It's just the stress of moving to a strange new place." She smiled at Maggie, but her face remained worried, her eyes puffy.

Maggie felt bad about waking her. Her mother had had a hard day.

"Think you can sleep now?" Mrs. Travers asked.

Maggie nodded. "Thanks," she murmured as her mother and sister left the room. "Uh, leave the door open," she added. She felt foolish saying that, but she hadn't gotten over the dream yet.

She couldn't shake her fear. It seemed to hover over her, hover over the canopy bed like a heavy cloud.

Maggie had set her alarm for seven. She wanted to get to the pool at the high school and swim for an hour before breakfast. Swimming was so relaxing. She could just get in the water, shut her mind off, and tell her body, "Swim!"

But when she opened her eyes, the clock radio said ten. She picked it up and examined it. It had stopped. The outlet she had plugged it into must be controlled by the light switch at the door. Ten was when she had turned out the light to go to bed.

She found her watch. It was nearly eleven.

"Oh, great," Maggie muttered unhappily. Another morning swim missed. And the next day was the first tryout for the All-State swim team.

Sighing, Maggie pulled on faded denim shorts and an oversize T-shirt, and hurried down for a late Sunday morning breakfast. Then she and Andrea spent the rest of the morning helping their mom dust and mop.

Maggie wasn't in the greatest of moods. She decided it would help if she set up her room the way she had in their old house. But that only made her sadder.

When she put up her old swimming posters, it made her notice how badly the off-white walls of her room needed a fresh coat of paint.

Then she lined up her crystal collection on the dresser. Her old room had been so sunny, the crystals changed colors constantly. Here, the prisms and glass animals barely shone.

As she worked in her room, Maggie found one other thing the previous owners had left behind. On the wide ledge outside her window sat a tiny potted geranium. Dead. The shriveled and gnarled plant seemed to sum up her mood.

Justin will cheer me up, she told herself.

Around two, she started to get nervous butterflies about seeing him. She told her mom to be sure to keep an ear out for the doorbell. She even went outside and pressed the doorbell, just to make sure it worked.

Then she took a quick shower and put on clean clothes—a fresh pair of faded denim jeans, a white T-shirt, and a green-checked vest she had found at a flea market. It brought out the green in her eyes.

She knocked on Andrea's door. "Come in," Andrea said lifelessly.

Maggie found her sprawled on her back in bed. "What's up?" Maggie asked her.

Andrea ignored the question. "We'll get used to this place, right?" she asked gloomily.

Maggie shrugged. She caught a glimpse of a fashion magazine tucked under Andrea's pillow. Andrea always claimed she didn't care about looks or fashion or anything superficial like that.

But once when Maggie was looking for a CD Andrea had borrowed, she came across a whole shoebox full of articles Andrea had clipped from women's magazines. Articles such as "10 Ways to Look Slimmer and Trimmer" and "Want to Look Tall? Stand Tall!" That kind of thing.

"I haven't found my hairbrush yet," Maggie moaned. "Can I borrow yours?"

"Go ahead."

Maggie found the silver hairbrush on Andrea's dresser and started brushing her wavy red hair in long strokes. "Justin will be here any minute," she told her sister.

In the mirror she caught the jealous expression that briefly flashed across Andrea's face.

What am I supposed to do? Maggie thought bitterly. Break up with Justin just so Andrea won't be jealous?

Maggie studied her sister's face, trying to think of some way to cheer her up. "You still feeling down about moving here?" she asked.

"I guess," Andrea murmured. "It's just weird. The house, the neighborhood." She swallowed hard, then added, "No Dad."

"I know," Maggie said softly. The silence was heavy between them. There wasn't anything else to say, and they both knew it.

"I've just been having such strange thoughts," Andrea confessed, avoiding her sister's eyes. "Strange, strange thoughts." She paused, then flashed Maggie a tense smile. "Have a good time with Justin," she said coldly.

"Where *is* he?" Maggie asked out loud, staring out the front window. It was four o'clock and no sign of Justin.

By five o'clock she swore to herself she was going to break up with him. How could he *do* this to her?

At ten after five, the doorbell finally rang. Maggie eagerly scrambled down the stairs. By the time she reached the bottom step, she wasn't angry anymore.

She opened the door to Justin standing there, one hand behind his back.

"Something for *me?*" Maggie asked delightedly.

Justin pulled his hand out. He was holding a big bag of kitchen sponges.

"How romantic!" Maggie said.

He caught her puzzled expression. "You said you had all this cleaning up to do," he explained, grinning.

"Oh, right."

Maggie stepped forward and gave him a quick

peck on the cheek, touching his arm softly. She had to stand on tiptoe to do it, which she liked.

Maggie was almost five feet eight. That meant she was usually as tall if not taller than her boyfriends. Justin was six feet, easy. And so great-looking, she felt like pinching herself.

"Look, Mom," Maggie said as she led Justin into the house. "New sponges."

Mrs. Travers melted as if Justin had brought her a bouquet of roses. "Just what I needed!" she gushed.

"Mom's a cheap date," Maggie said dryly.

"Hey, Mags," Justin said, glancing around, "this place isn't as bad as you said."

"You see?" Mrs. Travers beamed. Justin was really turning on the charm.

"You want something to drink?" Maggie asked as she led him to the kitchen. "We've got two cans of Sprite and"—she yanked open the fridge and peered inside—"and two cans of Sprite."

"We've got a little shopping to do," Mom explained guiltily.

"Uh, I think I'll have a Sprite," Justin said. His blue eyes twinkled. Maggie found herself staring at them. She couldn't help it. Justin's eyes were the color of the water in those ads for vacation islands in the Caribbean.

"Come on," she told him, handing him the can, "let me give you the grand tour."

It was a small house, so the tour didn't last long. They ended up in Maggie's room. Justin sat on the only chair. Maggie draped herself across the bed, hoping he would come sit next to her and kiss her.

He didn't.

They had already made out a couple of times, but their relationship was so new, it was as if they had to start from scratch each time they saw each other.

Just then, Gus bounded into the room and ran straight to Justin. If only I could be that direct! Maggie thought.

Gus collapsed on the floor, begging Justin to scratch his belly. Maggie laughed. On second thought, she told herself, I don't think I *do* want to be like Gus!

Justin scratched Gus with his sneaker. Gus whimpered with delight. Then he got up and trotted out of the room again, and the silent tension between Maggie and Justin returned.

"Are you all set for the tryouts tomorrow?" Justin asked finally.

Maggie groaned. "Thanks for reminding me."

"Why? You're not nervous, are you?"

"Not me." She jumped to her feet and began pacing.

"You'll do great," Justin promised.

"I hope so," Maggie replied. She didn't want to be superstitious, but compliments like that always made her feel that she was going to mess up.

Coach Randall was holding tryouts to decide who would swim the 200IM in the All-State meet. The 200IM was the Individual Medley, the most taxing event. The swimmer had to be good in every stroke.

Shadyside could enter only two swimmers in the event. Coach Randall had narrowed the field to four.

"My biggest competition is your old sweetheart, Dawn," Maggie said, making a face at him.

Justin grinned. "Sweetheart? Come on, Mags. Give me a break! I keep telling you, we went out once. One date!"

Maggie tried not to show how pleased she was by his answer. "Well, anyway, I think Dawn is going to beat me."

"Dawn's tough," Justin agreed.

"Oh, thanks for the support!" Maggie cried, laughing. "That was the wrong answer. You're supposed to tell me I can beat her easily. You're supposed to say I could lap her twice in a two-lap race!"

Justin's expression turned serious. "I think you can beat her," he said.

"You think?"

"I know."

"I feel so much better," she said, rolling her eyes. Actually, it did mean a lot to her that Justin had confidence in her abilities. When it came to sports, Justin knew a lot. He was captain of the Shadyside High baseball team and a track star.

"You know, Tiffany also has a shot," Justin added.

Tiffany Hollings was a soft-spoken girl with dark frizzy hair and large almond-shaped eyes. Maggie had learned not to take her for granted. Tiffany worked out for hours every day, including weekends. She had a fantastic dolphin kick and a gorgeous backstroke.

"And then there's Andrea," Maggie said.

37

Justin replied, "You can take Andrea, no prob."

Maggie turned quickly toward her bedroom door. "Shh!"

When she saw the coast was clear, she lowered her voice to a whisper. "That's not true. Don't write Andrea off. She's really getting good. And besides, beating me is her life's goal."

"That's because she's never done it," Justin replied.

Maggie sighed. "I'm so pumped, Justin. So totally pumped. I want to swim the Individual Medley so much that if I don't get it, I'll *kill* myself!"

"I'm glad you're not putting any extra pressure on yourself," Justin teased.

"There's something else," Maggie said. Justin waited, studying her with his perfect blue eyes. "I had a dream last night."

"Let me guess. You dreamed that when you walked into the pool, your bathing suit fell off and everyone was laughing at you. I have those dreams all the time before a big game."

"Wrong," she said, shaking her head. "There was a girl in my dream. I couldn't see her face, but I could tell she was in trouble."

"Weird," Justin replied. "But what does that have to do with swimming?"

"Nothing," she admitted. "But I keep thinking that maybe it's a bad omen."

"Nope," Justin said with a reassuring grin. "Just a bad dream."

To Maggie's surprise, Justin jumped up from his

chair. He put his strong hands on her shoulders. Then he kissed her on the lips.

A long, deep kiss. She felt his arms sweep around her and move down her back. She didn't know until that instant how much she had wanted to be held.

When the kiss ended, they were both breathless.

Maggie's heart was thudding in her chest. She gave Justin several quick kisses on the cheek.

Then she glanced past him to the bedroom doorway.

And saw that they were not alone.

Someone stood in the shadows, staring at them.

The girl from the dream!

chapter

5

Maggie gasped so loudly that Justin spun around in alarm.

"Andrea—hi!" he called.

Andrea?

Maggie squinted hard. Yes. It was Andrea.

Is she spying on Justin and me? Maggie thought angrily.

"Where's your camera? Do you want to take a picture?" Maggie demanded sarcastically.

"Huh?" Andrea pretended not to understand.

"How long were you standing there?" Maggie snapped.

Ignoring her sister's anger, Andrea stepped into the room. "I just wanted to see if you had unpacked any socks," she said. "I can't find mine. See?" She held up one bare foot, wiggling her toes.

She had painted her nails cherry red. She lifted her foot so high, she almost lost her balance.

Maggie continued to glare at her. That was a lie, and Andrea knew it. Socks! But she stalked to her dresser.

"I saw the home run you hit against Waynesbridge," Andrea told Justin, coyly lowering her head, too shy to look at him.

"What did you say?" Justin asked, distracted. "Oh, yeah, thanks."

Andrea was obviously stung. Maggie knew that being ignored by a guy like Justin was a million times more insulting than anything *she* could have said. "Here, catch," Maggie said. She tossed Andrea a rolled-up pair of white socks.

As soon as her sister left, Maggie closed the door.

"What's with her?" Justin asked.

"She hates me," Maggie answered.

"She's just jealous," Justin said. He slipped his hands around Maggie's waist, pulling her toward him.

She stepped back. "You know, when I saw her standing there in the doorway, it reminded me of my dream again."

"Yeah?" Justin reached for her again, but she moved away.

She sat down in the chair, where he couldn't get to her. Andrea had shaken her up and totally destroyed her romantic mood. She needed to talk.

"Justin," she said thoughtfully. "I know this sounds dumb. But I've never had a bad dream that scared me before. I can't help thinking, what if the dream is a warning?"

"What kind of warning?"

She shrugged, feeling the same fright she had the night before. "I don't know. Just a warning. A warning that something bad is going to happen."

"Forget about it. Nothing bad is going to happen," Justin assured her. "You're just tense, Mags, because of moving and because—"

He stopped in mid-sentence, his breath caught in his throat.

His eyes went wide in sudden fright, his mouth hanging open. He grabbed his chest.

"Justin?" Maggie cried shrilly.

His hands went up to his throat. He uttered a hoarse choking sound and staggered toward her.

Another choking sound. "Can't—breathe—"

Before Maggie could get to him, Justin had crumpled lifelessly to the floor.

chapter

6

Maggie stood over him. "Justin? Justin?"

Then she gave him a little kick when she noticed his stomach moving up and down.

"You jerk!" she cried. "You scared me to death!"

He grabbed her ankle and let out a high-pitched hyena laugh.

"I didn't believe you for a second!" Maggie exclaimed.

"Liar!" he cried. "You fell for it! You nearly had a cow!"

"You're not funny!" She nudged him again.

A few seconds later they were laughing and wrestling playfully on the carpet. "Thanks for cheering me up!" Maggie cried.

She pinned both his shoulders to the floor, then jumped to her feet, cheering victoriously.

43

"Give me a break! How about two out of three?"
Justin demanded.

Dawn Rodgers slipped her long, tanned arms
through the straps of her black Speedo racing suit
and flicked the material into position. "Okay, everybody, ready to take a lesson?" she called.

Dawn whooped out a war cry. The cry echoed off
the walls of the half-empty locker room.

"Please spare us, Dawn," Tiffany Hollings
moaned, clutching her ears. "We won't be able to
hear the starting whistle."

Dawn laughed. "You'll hear it all right. And here's
the next thing you'll hear." She cupped her hand
into a microphone. "Now swimming the two-
hundred IM for Shadyside, in lane number one—
Dawwwwwnnn Rodgers!"

Maggie was sitting on the bench next to Dawn,
braiding her hair and smiling broadly. Imitating an
announcer's voice, she added, "But what's this?
Dawn's wearing her tennis whites! Oh, no—those
are definitely going to slow her down."

Dawn, Maggie, and Tiffany laughed at that. Only
Andrea, who had been scrabbling through her locker
in the corner, didn't seem to hear.

Coach Randall had asked the four girls to come to
practice fifteen minutes early, so they could race
while they were still fresh. The locker door opened
just then, and Carly Pedersen, Claudia Walker, and
Renee Larson, all members of the swim team,
strolled in. "Hey, you guys, good luck today!" Carly
called.

Maggie grinned and waved, but her heart did a flip turn. That's what it felt like, anyway.

In competitive swimming, the racer somersaulted at the end of each lap, pushing off the wall with her feet. It was called a flip turn. About five minutes before every race, Maggie's heart and stomach started doing flip turns.

"Okay, okay," Andrea suddenly said, and slammed her locker shut. "Let's have it, Maggie."

Maggie turned to her sister in surprise. "Have what?"

"My bathing cap. Where did you hide it?"

Unbelievable! Maggie thought. Andrea was always accusing her of things. "Did you lose it?" Maggie asked.

"Did I lose it?" Andrea mimicked nastily. "Very funny. Hand it over."

Everyone in the locker room was staring at them. "Andrea," Maggie said as patiently as she could, "I didn't take it." She bent into her locker. "Here, maybe I have an extra one."

"I don't want an *extra* one. I want mine," Andrea insisted.

Andrea had dumped most of her stuff on the floor. Tiffany pointed to something white sticking out from under Andrea's backpack. "Is that it?"

Andrea yanked the backpack away, revealing her bathing cap. "Oh—yeah," she mumbled, red-faced.

Some of the other girls in the locker room started giggling, which only made Andrea blush harder. Maggie turned away. Even when Andrea was acting like a spoiled brat, she didn't want to see her get teased.

Tiffany finished dressing and started some warm-up stretches. "I think I'm going to hurl!" she declared as she bent her head toward the floor.

"You're that stressed out?" Dawn asked. "Relax. You have nothing to worry about. You always swim great. Besides, we're all on the same team, right?"

"That's right," agreed Maggie, glancing at Andrea.

The locker room door swung open, and Coach Randall walked in, carrying her clipboard.

Martha Randall was tall and stick-thin, even thinner than Maggie. As a teenage swimmer, she had once made it all the way to the Olympic trials. Now she was in her forties, and she still had the intensity of a champion. It was a quality Maggie really admired.

Coach Randall rarely said much. Today was no exception. "Okay, the four girls for the two-hundred IM," she said, studying her clipboard. "Let's go."

This was the one part of swimming that Maggie hated, the time just before she got in the water. She knew she'd be all right once the race started. But now she was starting to feel dizzy as they padded barefoot through the long hallway that led to the pool.

The familiar smell of steam and chlorine swept over her. The pool gurgled softly, the water slapping gently against the sides.

"Good luck," Maggie murmured to Andrea.

Maggie glanced at the bleachers. A few of her

teammates had pulled on their suits and come out to watch. They waved and Maggie waved back.

Dawn was right, Maggie told herself. Why should I feel so nervous? I've raced against these three girls in practice all year.

"Let's get started," Coach Randall said curtly. She checked her clipboard. "Tiffany, lane one; Andrea, two; Maggie, three; Dawn, four."

The four girls bent over and scooped up water to splash on their bodies. Then they took their places on the starting blocks.

Before Maggie pulled her goggles on, she spat into them to moisten the rubber edge. She always did this, to make sure the seal was watertight. But this time she had trouble spitting. Her mouth was dry.

Nervous, nervous, she scolded herself.

She glanced at Andrea. Her sister was staring straight ahead with an expression of cold determination.

On Maggie's right, Dawn was nervously flexing her hands. She had known Dawn Rodgers long enough to know that her confident manner was mostly an act. Dawn was as worried about the race as Maggie was.

"Okay, this is the two-hundred IM," Coach Randall reminded them. "Butterfly, backstroke, breaststroke, freestyle—in that order, two lengths each. Any questions?"

No one had any, except for the one question they were all silently asking: Who will win?

* * *

Coach Randall moved into a crouch to watch the race and judge the finish.

Maggie shook her head, trying to clear it. She had so many stray thoughts flying around—Andrea, the new house, Justin. . . .

She knew if she wanted a shot at winning this race, she was going to have to concentrate. Focus! she told herself. Focus!

Below her, the water stretched, blue, still, and cold. The four girls lowered themselves into a diving crouch.

Coach Randall called out, "On your mark, get set—" Then the whistle blew shrilly.

Maggie dove.

She hit the water, glided up to the surface, kicking hard.

The key to the butterfly was the rhythm of the dolphin kick. Maggie tried to picture the grace and strength of a dolphin diving in and out of the water.

Before she knew it, the first length had ended. Maggie tucked and somersaulted.

A perfect flip turn.

She could tell she was in first place.

Concentrate! Concentrate!

Maybe she had started too fast. It was only the second length, and she was feeling tired, slowing down.

Concentrate!

Halfway through the first length of the backstroke, Maggie saw Dawn pass her on the right. Then Andrea started edging by on her left. There was no way to know where Tiffany was, since she was two lanes away.

So much for her early lead! The coach was screaming instructions, and her teammates were screaming encouragement.

But their voices were only a jumbled echo. "Dig! Dig!" was the only thing Maggie picked up.

Breaststroke next.

Maggie was breathing hard now, and every muscle ached.

But the thought of losing hurt a lot more.

She silently commanded herself: *Faster! Faster!*

She pushed harder, harder—as she came to the end of the breaststroke. But then she made a poor turn at the wall.

I've blown it! she thought.

She had never lost a really big race before.

Could she still win? It was now or never.

Freestyle was her strongest stroke. But she had only two laps to catch up.

She felt as if she were skimming over the water. The shrill cheers and screams in the gym reached an even higher pitch. Nearing the far wall, Maggie passed Andrea—then Tiffany.

Maggie kept charging. She was swimming very close to the lane marker, but there was no time to straighten out now. She just had to hope that her hand didn't smack into the little lane markers, or she'd lose for sure.

Faster! Faster!

She pulled herself forward, churning through the

water with all her might. She was only inches behind Dawn now.

Only a few strokes left.

She pulled with all her might and stretched for the wall.

Her wet palm slapped the tiles—

And a split second later—

Dawn hit the wall.

Maggie was first.

Tiffany arrived a full second later.

And a stroke behind her—Andrea, who finished fourth.

Holding on to the wall with both hands and gasping for breath, Maggie gazed up at Coach Randall with a happy grin. The coach was studying her stopwatch and making notes on the clipboard.

"First place, Maggie Travers," she called. Maggie didn't bother to listen to the rest, she just pushed off the wall into a lazy backstroke as she started to unwind.

Then she swam back and dragged herself out of the pool. After swimming so hard, her arms ached and her body felt like dead weight.

"Nice finish, Maggie," Coach Randall told her, and smiled.

Maggie beamed. Compliments from Coach Randall were like gold.

"Next time I want to see you pick up the pace on your butterfly and backstroke," the coach added.

She never let you have a pure compliment. There was always a catch.

"Whoa! Time out!" Dawn cried. She was out of

the pool now and charging over to Maggie and the coach. "There was interference! Didn't you see it? Maggie shoved the line right into me."

"She didn't shove the line," Coach Randall replied firmly. "Her wake pushed the line over."

"Well, so what?" Dawn continued. "You're not going to allow that, are you?"

"Save it, Dawn," Coach Randall replied sharply. "You came in second."

Andrea picked up a towel and wrapped it around her broad shoulders. Maggie gave her a sympathetic glance. Andrea turned away.

Some congratulations!

Tiffany sat on the edge of the pool, kicking her feet in the water, shaking her head unhappily.

"Okay, girls," Coach Randall said with a smile. "Let's not get down. That was just one race. We've got three more."

Maggie glanced up to see Dawn glaring at her, breathing hard. "Dawn," Maggie said, "I'm sorry. I didn't mean to—"

"Of course not," Dawn replied, rolling her eyes.

Maggie glimpsed Andrea watching them, obviously enjoying the argument.

"All right," Coach Randall called to the girls in the bleachers. "Everyone in the pool!"

Maggie groaned. The race had been so intense. She had forgotten they still had an hour of practice!

By the time practice was over, Maggie was exhausted. Every muscle ached.

She took a really long shower.

Some girls talked excitedly about the practice and

the races. But Maggie dressed in silence, lost in her own thoughts.

She was the last one out of the locker room.

She walked out through the pool.

Most of the lights were off now. Maggie's eyes were still burning from the chlorine. They kept blurring, watering over.

So it wasn't until she got right up to the water that she saw the body floating facedown in the pool.

chapter
7

"*D*awn!" Maggie shrieked.

In the middle of the pool Dawn's body was slowly drifting with the water's gentle movement.

Maggie hesitated for only a second. Then she dove into the water with all her clothes on.

Please—let me be in time! Maggie prayed. Please!

When she surfaced, Dawn was still several yards away.

Please—be alive! Be alive! Maggie prayed.

Dawn raised her head.

"Dawn!" Maggie gasped, swimming over and grabbing her.

Dawn's face twisted in surprise. "Let go," she said, shoving Maggie away. "What's your problem?"

Maggie treaded water, staring at her in disbelief. "*My* problem? What do you think *you're* doing?"

Dawn blinked water from her eyes. "Practicing breath control, what do you think?"

53

"I—I thought you were dead!" Maggie stammered. She grabbed Dawn's arm again. It was hard to tread water with her clothes weighing her down.

Dawn laughed. "Dead?"

Maggie started laughing too, partly from relief and partly from embarrassment.

"I guess I got you," Dawn said, splashing water at Maggie's head.

"You did this on purpose, didn't you!" Maggie demanded, splashing Dawn back.

Dawn backstroked out of Maggie's splashing range. "No way!" she insisted. "How was I supposed to know you'd be such a jerk! Look at you! You've got all your clothes on!"

Maggie reluctantly admitted to herself that it was pretty funny.

Dawn threw her head back, laughing. She had a contagious laugh, and soon Maggie felt herself losing it as well. The two girls laughed till they nearly cried, their voices echoing off the high tile ceiling.

Tuesday night. Maggie struggled to fall asleep.

Staring up at the canopy over her head, she tried to clear her mind, to relax her muscles, to relax—relax.

As her eyes closed, she felt a force pulling her down.

It was as if she were being dragged down into the darkness.

A darkness that became a swirling gray haze.

As the haze circled around her, she drifted lower. Down toward a square of pink.

Focus! Focus! The square of pink became a canopy on an old-fashioned four-poster.

Under the canopy, Maggie could hear someone in the bed. Someone moaning, "No—no—"

Maggie drifted down through the pink canopy. Into the bed.

She saw the girl, who was tossing fitfully beneath pink blankets.

The girl with the ash-blond hair.

Maggie knew she was dreaming, but somehow that made the dream twice as frightening.

It was cold in the room, but there were beads of sweat glistening on the girl's bare shoulders. She lay still now, her head turned away.

If only Maggie could see her face!

Maggie wanted to call to the girl to turn around. But when she opened her mouth, no sound came out.

This girl was in trouble. Maggie knew it.

And then she knew why. It came over her suddenly, like a shadow rolling across her body.

She and the girl were not alone. There was someone else in the room!

Maggie whirled. And saw—

The glint of a knife blade in the darkness!

Then all at once the darkness exploded violently as a figure leaped forward.

The blond girl tried to twist away. And her skull smacked against the headboard. Then the knife came slashing down through the air.

Maggie jerked so sharply in her sleep that she

woke herself up. She lay in her bed in the darkness, gasping in air, her heart thudding, her eyes still shut.

Just a dream, she told herself. Just a dream, just a dream, just a—

An image from the nightmare loomed in her mind. The pink canopy! The same pink canopy she saw when she opened her eyes. The canopy. *Her* canopy.

The girl in the dream was sleeping in *her* bed!

The realization made Maggie's heart start to pound even harder. What did it mean?

I'm just stressed out, she told herself, gripping the bedsheet. I'm sleeping in a new bed. So I'm dreaming about it. That's all.

But then another frightening thought came to her—one she'd had before. Maybe the dream was a warning. Maybe her own subconscious mind was trying to warn her about something through the dream.

But what? *What?*

She closed her eyes and rolled over onto her side, gazing at the window.

Only then did Maggie feel the presence of the intruder. Her eyes popped open. Her mouth contorted into a silent scream.

The girl stood blanketed in darkness next to Maggie's bed, staring straight down at her, straight down into her face.

With a desperate gasp, Maggie jerked backward, banging her head against the headboard.

She couldn't get away.

The girl reached out to grab her.

chapter

8

Maggie opened her mouth to scream.

"It's me, it's me, it's me!" the girl kept repeating in a desperate whisper.

Maggie stopped yelling and covered her mouth, her shoulders heaving.

The girl leaned closer, close enough for Maggie to see her face. "Andrea!"

"Are you okay?" Andrea's features showed her concern.

"Andrea!" Maggie murmured. "I keep thinking you're the one in the dream. I keep mistaking you—Why?"

Andrea squeezed Maggie's hand. "You're not making any sense. Get yourself together, Maggie. You're *scaring* me."

"S-sorry," Maggie stammered. She pulled herself up and shook her head as if trying to shake the dream away.

"You were moaning and making all these frightening cries," Andrea whispered. "I thought I'd better wake you."

Maggie swallowed hard. Her mouth was dry. She covered her face with her hands. "Wow."

"Another nightmare?" Andrea asked, settling down on the edge of the bed.

"No," Maggie replied through her hands. "Same one I had the other night. Only this time—"

"What?"

Maggie shut her eyes, picturing the dream again. "This time the girl got stabbed! It was so awful. She was being stabbed, and I—I couldn't do anything about it."

"Who stabbed her?" Andrea asked.

"I don't know. I couldn't see."

"It's like a horror movie," Andrea said.

"Yeah. Only it's playing right in my head."

They sat in silence for a moment. Not total silence. The rickety old house was full of quiet sounds—creaks and cracks.

"Did my cries wake you?" Maggie asked, her voice still shaky.

"Nah," Andrea said. "I was up. I couldn't sleep. I went downstairs for a glass of water—and guess where Gus is sleeping?"

"Next to the rocking chair?"

Andrea nodded.

"Dumb old Gus," Maggie murmured affectionately.

Officially, Gus was Maggie's dog. But really, Gus had been Mr. Travers's dog. Wherever Mr. Travers was, that was where you'd find Gus, sleeping with his head on Mr. Travers's lap or feet.

Mr. Travers liked to read in the rocking chair at night, and so that was still Gus's favorite spot to snooze.

From somewhere in the house came the sound of something snapping. Maggie jumped.

"Relax, will you?" Andrea cried. "You're getting *me* scared."

"I hate this house," Maggie admitted suddenly.

"You're not the only one."

"I feel like it's haunted."

"Please," Andrea begged. "I'll be up all night."

"No, you won't. You're not the one having nightmares."

"Maggie, you've got to calm down. Don't start losing it. It's only a dream."

Maggie wasn't listening. In her head the dream started to replay itself. Something was bothering her—teasing at the edges of her memory.

What was it? What was she trying to picture? She couldn't quite get a hold on it.

Andrea stood up. She ran her finger down one of the bedposts. "See? I told you you should've let me have this bed. It's bad luck. And it's giving you nightmares."

Maggie stared at her as if she hadn't heard. "The bed . . ." she said. That was it! She reached out and grabbed her sister's hand. "Andrea, you're right! The girl in the dream, the girl in trouble? She was sleeping in this bed!"

"That's spooky," Andrea admitted. "And she got . . ."

She let the question trail off. Maggie finished it for her. "Stabbed," she murmured softly. "With a knife. Over and over. Don't you see? I *knew* it was too good to be true," Maggie moaned unhappily.

"What was?"

"The owners just leaving this beautiful bed behind. There had to be something wrong with it."

Andrea shook her head. "This isn't like you, Maggie."

"Something is wrong here," Maggie whispered, thinking out loud. "I can feel it."

"Did you see the girl's face this time?" Andrea asked.

Maggie shook her head. "No."

"Hmm. What does she look like?"

"She has long blond hair. Ash blond."

"Ash blond," Andrea repeated thoughtfully.

"Why?" Maggie asked nervously. "You know who she is?"

"No," Andrea said with a smile. "I was just thinking, I have *no idea* who she is."

Maggie waited for Andrea to explain.

"Well, this'll sound crazy," Andrea continued. "But you want to know what I think is giving you nightmares?"

"What?"

"You're putting yourself under too much pressure with the swim team. It's like you *have* to be number one or else."

Maggie frowned. "So? I want to do well. What's wrong with that?"

"Nothing. Don't get defensive."

"I'm not getting defensive," Maggie insisted.

"Well, that's all I'm saying," Andrea said. "I just think that could be what's causing this. Maybe with Dad, and the move to this house, and the competition—it's all too much for your brain. It's on overload."

"What does swimming have to do with a girl getting stabbed?" Maggie demanded, her voice rising.

Andrea shrugged, as if the connection were obvious. "Maybe you want to stab the rest of us so you'll be the winner."

"That—that is totally stupid!" Maggie protested.

"Okay, okay," Andrea said quickly. "Forget I brought it up. I'm no shrink. How am *I* supposed to know what your dumb dream means?"

Maggie regretted raising her voice. Andrea was only trying to help. "Who knows," Maggie said. "Maybe it *is* the swim team that's got me so stressed. But what am I supposed to do? Drop swimming because I had a couple of nightmares?"

"No, but you could ease up a little. Not push yourself quite so hard," Andrea suggested.

Maggie laughed scornfully. "Right. Take it easy. So you can swim the two-hundred IM instead of me, right?"

Instantly, Andrea's eyes became dark with anger.

Uh-oh, Maggie thought. What did I say?

"You really are disgusting!" Andrea cried, shaking her head bitterly. "No matter what I do, you always think the worst of me, don't you?"

"Andrea, what are you talking about? I—"

"You think I said that because I want to beat you in swimming? You think this was all some kind of trick?"

"No, Andrea, I was just jok—"

"Believe me, Maggie, swimming isn't all I think about. Get a life!"

"I didn't say you did, I just—"

Andrea stabbed the air with her forefinger to stress her point. "I don't need tricks to beat you. Because I can swim faster and better than you. How do you like that?"

Maggie sighed. "Andrea," she said. "You're taking this all wrong. I didn't mean—"

Andrea was on her feet now. "Don't do that," she snarled.

"Don't do *what?*"

"Don't start acting all innocent and sweet after you insult me. You always do this. Always!"

"Always do *what?*"

"You make a crack," Andrea said. "And then when I get mad, you pretend you have no idea why I'm angry, so *I'll* look crazy."

"Andrea, you *are* crazy!" Maggie cried in frustration. "You're making up this whole fight out of nothing."

"Right," Andrea snapped. "It's all my fault. It's always all my fault. You're Miss Perfect. Right?"

Maggie raised her hands helplessly. "Did I say that?"

"I came in here because I was worried about you," Andrea said, her voice trembling. "I came in because you sounded upset. And this is the thanks I get!"

"Please, Andrea," Maggie said. "Look how angry you are because of one stupid remark I made about the swim team. What's the big deal here? You and I both know that you don't exactly wish me the best of luck on the swim team."

"And what about you?" Andrea cried furiously. "Who's the one dreaming about a girl getting stabbed, huh? Dreams are all *wishes,* right? That's what I learned in psych class. So who do you want to stab? Who do you want to be dead? Who?"

Was Andrea right? Maggie wondered, suddenly cold all over.

She couldn't be.

The dream *can't* be telling me I want to stab someone.

It *can't* be telling me I'm *going* to stab someone!

Because when I'm in the dream, Maggie realized, I'm not on the side of the attacker. I don't identify with the attacker.

I identify with the *victim!*

chapter
9

Maggie spun the dial on her combination lock for the third time. What was wrong with her? She couldn't focus her eyes.

Was it left to 22? Or right? She ought to know. She had only opened her lock about a zillion times.

She pulled down hard, and the lock finally popped open. She loaded her history and math books onto the top shelf.

It was Friday. TGIF, thought Maggie wearily. Why was she so tired? Because she hadn't been sleeping well.

Every night when she went to bed, she worried about dreaming again. The dream hadn't returned. But the thought of having it scared her so much, she tossed and turned every night. Every sound in the house became amplified and scary. She hadn't had a good night's sleep since they moved to Fear Street.

Maggie shoved her English textbook far into the

locker. The assignment for that day had been to read a story about a boy who keeps thinking it's snowing. Turns out there is no snow. It's all in his head. He's going insane.

Just what I needed to read! she told herself sarcastically.

She pulled out her notebook for Mrs. Harrison's geology class, snapped her lock closed, and followed the stream of students through the noisy hallway. Only one more period to go.

And then she had swim. She was so tired, her feet felt like lead. Forget finishing first in any race. She'd probably sink straight to the bottom of the pool!

Geology class was down one flight. She joined the crowd in the stairwell. Sunlight streamed in through the tall windows of the hallway. It caught a flash of red hair up ahead.

"Andrea!" she called.

She hurried to catch up to her sister. There was no way to push through, and her voice was drowned out by the loud conversation and laughter.

Then, a few yards ahead, she saw Dawn, laughing happily as she started down the stairs with a couple of guys on the basketball team.

"Excuse me, excuse me—" Maggie forced her way forward.

She had no idea why. She suddenly felt very uneasy. She pushed harder. "Hey," someone said. "Watch it. No shoving!"

Her heart started to pound. Why was she feeling so strange?

"Dawn!" she called again.

Moving with the crowd, Maggie now started down the stairs too.

"Hey—Dawn! *Oh!*" Maggie cried out as she saw Dawn start to lose her footing.

She heard a sharp cry.

And saw Dawn start to fall.

It all happened in an instant, but that one instant seemed to go on endlessly, as if the whole world had gone into slow motion.

Dawn tumbled forward, down the concrete stairs.

Her books flew out in front of her.

Her head bounced on the concrete with a deafening *crack*—louder than the startled shrieks and cries of the crowd.

Another loud *crack* as she finished rolling and hit the floor.

Her legs twisted under her.

Her jaw fell open lifelessly. Her eyes stared blankly.

Dawn didn't move.

chapter

10

Maggie's Trapper Keeper fell from her arms and bumped down the stairs. She raised her hands to her eyes to shut out the ugly picture of her friend lying twisted at the bottom of the stairs.

"Dawn—Dawn—" she muttered.

The stairwell echoed with shouts and cries. A crowd had circled around Dawn.

From near the top of the stairs, Maggie saw Dawn begin to writhe in agony. "My arm!" Dawn screamed. "It— I think it's broken!"

"Get a teacher!" somebody yelled. "Somebody— call 911!"

Kids took off in all directions. Maggie heard frantic cries for help.

Someone tried to help Dawn sit up. But she shrieked in pain when she was touched.

"My arm—my arm—" she cried shrilly. "Somebody pushed me!"

Maggie took a deep breath and made her way down the stairs, gripping the railing tightly. She spotted Andrea at the outside of the circle.

Andrea turned and gazed at Maggie. She had the strangest expression on her face. Half smile, half bitter stare.

"Dawn, are you okay?" Maggie asked. "What happened? Did you trip?"

Dawn's reply made Maggie turn away. "No. I told you. I was pushed. Did you do it? Did you push me?" Dawn cried through her tears.

"Huh?" Maggie wasn't sure she had heard correctly.

"Maggie—" Dawn insisted weakly, her arm bent behind her, tears flowing down her pale cheeks. "I heard you call me, Maggie. Then—then you pushed me."

Horrified, Maggie started to sputter. "Huh? Dawn —no! I—I couldn't! I wasn't near you. I mean—"

Maggie turned to Andrea for help. But Andrea was staring down at the floor. "Tell her I didn't do this, Andrea," Maggie begged.

"I—I didn't see anything," Andrea stammered.

All around her, Maggie felt the accusing stares of the other students. Maggie glared back at them in disbelief. Did they really think she would push someone down the stairs? Didn't they know her better than that?

With an angry sob, she picked up her Trapper Keeper, turned, and pushed her way back up the stairs. No one made it easy for her to pass.

By the time Maggie reached the upstairs hallway, she was crying. Fighting back her tears, she started to run.

The final bell rang for class. But Maggie ran straight into the girls' room. She shut the door hard and leaned against it. At least she was alone.

She turned and saw her tear-stained face in the mirror.

The dream. As she stared at herself, the dream popped into her head.

Dawn has blond hair. The girl in the dream has blond hair.

Andrea had guessed the girl might be Dawn the first time she heard about her.

And in the dream, the girl always fell backward, smacking her head hard against the headboard. Dawn had just smacked her head against the concrete, just like the girl in her dream.

In the mirror, Maggie saw her own eyes widen with fear, and the tight-lipped horror on her own face scared her even more.

Was the dream coming true?

Andrea's words came back to her: *Dreams were wishes.*

Could Maggie have caused Dawn's accident somehow? Even without meaning to?

She made it through geology class, but her mind was somewhere else the whole time. Mrs. Harrison was going through plans for the field trip scheduled for the next Wednesday.

About a forty-five-minute ride out of Shadyside was Glenn Rock Mountain. The caverns at Glenn Rock were a popular tourist attraction.

Maggie didn't really listen to what Mrs. Harrison was saying. Halfway through the period, she asked to be excused to go check on Dawn.

Maggie went to the principal's office. The news didn't cheer her up. Dawn had a broken arm. And possibly a concussion.

After school, Maggie ran into Tiffany in the hallway. "Do you *believe* what happened to Dawn?" Tiffany asked quietly. "She could've been killed!"

"Tiffany—you've *got* to believe me! I didn't do it!" Maggie blurted out.

Surprised, Tiffany studied her with her large eyes. "I never thought you did."

Maggie gratefully squeezed Tiffany's hand. Tiffany lowered her eyes. "Listen. Dawn had a concussion. She wasn't thinking clearly. That's why she accused you. She'll be better—don't worry."

"I hope so," Maggie replied, shaking her head, trying not to cry again. "It was so awful, Tiffany. Everyone was shoving. You know how it is on the stairs between classes. I'm sure it was just an accident."

"Of course," Tiffany replied. "But you can understand where Dawn's coming from. I mean, you have a pretty good reason to want her out of the way."

"Tiffany," Maggie said, trying to keep the sound of pleading out of her voice, "you know me better than that. Do you really think I'd hurt Dawn just to make sure I swim the two-hundred IM?"

Tiffany tugged at a strand of hair. "Of course not. Besides, you'll be in. Unless you totally blow the next three races. Anyway, there are *two* slots."

"So I had no reason to push Dawn," Maggie insisted. "Why did she accuse me? How *could* she? I'm so hurt, Tiffany. So hurt."

Tiffany moved forward to give Maggie an awkward hug. "Just give Dawn a little time," she whispered. "She'll come to her senses. Just give her a little time."

Maggie forced a smile. The two girls backed away from each other.

Maggie wiped a tear off her cheek.

Tiffany was right, she knew. Maggie would have to wait to talk to Dawn.

Maggie couldn't face swim practice. She told the coach she was sick and went straight home.

As soon as she got there, she threw herself facedown onto the living room couch. She didn't want to think anymore. She was just tired, worn out. She needed to rest.

That was the last thought she remembered. When she opened her eyes again, the room had grown darker.

Maggie groaned and sat up. She felt as if her brain were glued to her skull. The nap had made her disoriented and groggy. At least she hadn't had the nightmare.

Then she smelled tomato sauce, heard it bubbling softly in the kitchen. Her mother came into view, in the kitchen archway, holding a wooden spoon. She waved the spoon and smiled. "You were sleep-

71

ing when I got home from work. Dinner's almost ready. Your favorite. Spaghetti with nonmeat meatballs."

It wasn't *exactly* Maggie's favorite. She liked *real* meatballs. But Mrs. Travers was mainly a vegetarian.

"You were sleeping so peacefully, I didn't want to disturb you," her mother called. "The phone rang twice and you stayed dead to the world. I think you really needed the sleep, Maggie."

Sleeping peacefully—for once! It was the first time that Maggie had slept well in the new house. What made this time different?

She knew the answer right away. She had slept on the couch—not in the canopy bed.

That night, she stood in her bedroom, staring at the beautiful old bed. She still had not been able to figure out why the owners had left it behind.

Could it be because the bed was haunted?

How her feelings about this bed had changed since they first moved in! That first day, it had been the one good thing about having to move. She had loved it.

Now she feared it.

The backyard of 23 Fear Street was tiny, hemmed in by the lawns of three different houses. The previous owner had started a flagstone walk from the back door but had abandoned the project after laying only a few stones.

There was a rusty old swing set with two swings.

Maggie sat on one. It was designed for a young kid, and she had to stretch her long legs straight out in front of her to swing at all. The rusty chains creaked overhead as she rocked back and forth.

It was Saturday morning. A hot, sunny day with small puffs of white cloud high in a blue sky.

Usually Maggie woke up feeling refreshed, ready to go. But now she felt as tired as when she'd gone to bed.

She'd been up all night—thinking about Dawn, thinking about the dream, and wondering if there was any connection.

Inside the house, she saw her mother moving in her bedroom. Maggie waved and tried to smile.

She got off the swing and started making her way along the row of scrawny shrubs that bordered the yard. She pulled off a few early red berries and squished them in her fingers, making a bloody pulp.

Come on, she scolded herself. You've *got* to shake this. Think about something else.

But that was hopeless. She couldn't switch her mind off. What was the old game? You told someone not to think about an elephant. And then she couldn't think of anything else!

She sat down and leaned back against the smooth trunk of a white birch tree. Gazing up, she could see the sky through the budding branches. A gentle wind blew the clouds slowly by.

So peaceful. So quiet.

Before long, Maggie fell asleep.

73

A restful sleep with no disturbing dreams. No knives. No girl in pink.

And then a hand on her shoulder. She opened her eyes with a startled gasp.

And saw a frightening-looking man reaching for her throat. "This won't take long," he rasped.

chapter
11

Maggie pulled away with a terrified cry.

The man jerked back, his gray eyes wide with surprise.

"Sorry. Didn't mean to scare you," he said. "I—I asked if you've been baking long?" He pointed up at the sky. The late morning sun was climbing higher, heating up the backyard.

"You could get a bad burn today, even though it's spring," the man said. "I thought I'd better wake you."

"Uh—thanks," Maggie choked out. As she stared up at him, he came into sharper focus.

He was old, with a heavy white stubble on his leathery, creased face. He wore a battered orange cap and had a toothpick wedged in his mouth. His smile revealed uneven yellow teeth.

He held a hand out. It took Maggie a while to

realize he was offering to help her up. Reluctantly, she took his hand and climbed to her feet.

I am so jumpy and stressed out, she thought, scolding herself. I think everyone in the world is out to get me!

"Milton Avery," the old man said in his harsh voice. He nodded and raised two fingers to his cap. "I'm your neighbor."

He held out his right hand to Maggie. Maggie shook it. The old man held on to her hand a moment longer than Maggie would have liked. His skin felt like old paper.

"You haven't told me *your* name," Mr. Avery said.

"Oh, sorry. Maggie. Maggie Travers."

"Maggie Travers," the man repeated. He nodded thoughtfully. "Nice name."

Maggie smiled. "Thanks."

The man smiled back warmly. He removed his cap, revealing a head that was bald except for a fringe of scraggly white hair. He scratched the top of his head, then put the cap back on. He looked up at the house. "It sure is nice to have this house occupied again."

Maggie stared at the house too, as if she hadn't seen her own house before.

"It was on the market a long time," Mr. Avery said.

Maggie felt her spine tingle. "Was it?"

"A *long* time." The way he said it, Maggie wanted to ask just how long he meant. Years? Decades? He obviously could remember back a long way.

Mr. Avery went on. "I didn't like having an empty

house next door. Kind of gave me a dead feeling every time I saw it. Know what I mean?"

Maggie knew exactly what he meant.

Mr. Avery took his cap off again and used it to point at his house. "I even took to keeping the shades down on this side of the house. So I wouldn't have to see yours."

Maggie glanced at the still-drawn shades as another thought rolled through her mind. "Did you know the people who used to live in my house?" she asked.

Mr. Avery didn't answer right away. "Not really. They didn't live here very long. Terrible story. Terrible."

Her heart pounded hard. "Why—what?"

The old man searched her face. "The real estate salesman didn't tell you the story?"

"No, what story?"

Mr. Avery frowned. "Well, I guess I can't blame him for keeping it from you. I mean, Bob Jamison is a pretty honest guy, for a salesman, anyway. But he hadn't been able to sell this house for months. I guess he figured that if you didn't ask, he didn't have to tell."

He cleared his throat. His eyes focused on hers, boring into her. They were old eyes, pale gray, but clear and hard.

"Listen," he said hoarsely. "My wife, Claire, would sure love to meet you. A pretty young girl like you would brighten up her morning. She could use that. Why don't you come on over for a cup of tea, and I'll tell you the whole story."

Maggie glanced up at her house again to see if her

mom was watching. But her bedroom window was dark. "That sounds great," she said.

Mr. Avery pointed to a break in the hedge. "This way," he told her. He took off his cap, bowed, and gestured. "After you."

Mr. Avery's house was warm and cozy. There were family photos on the walls—children, grandchildren.

Mrs. Avery was sitting at the kitchen table, the newspaper folded beside her plate as she worked the daily crossword. She had a round moon face, accentuated by a halo of thin white hair. "I thought you were going to do some gardening, Milton," she said without looking up.

"I am, Claire," he said. "But as you can see—"

Mrs. Avery raised her eyes and smiled warmly.

"This is our new neighbor," Mr. Avery explained, placing a hand on Maggie's shoulder. "Claire, this is Martha—"

"Maggie," she corrected him.

"Maggie. Sorry. Maggie Travers."

Mrs. Avery stood up and smiled broadly. She shuffled over to shake Maggie's hand. "Welcome to the neighborhood," she said. "Oh, I'm so glad to meet you. Such a pretty girl. Are those green eyes?"

"Yes," Maggie replied uncomfortably.

"Gorgeous," Mrs. Avery said, nodding her head in admiration. "Oh, it must be nice to be young."

It hadn't been nice this week, that was for sure. "Mr. Avery said he was going to tell me—" Maggie started.

"Would you like some tea?" Mr. Avery interrupted. "And a gingersnap. Do we have any left, Claire?"

Claire moved to the stove, hefted the kettle to make sure there was water inside, then turned on the burner full blast. "I don't know," she said. "Check the cookie jar."

Maggie couldn't wait any longer. "What happened in my house?" she asked bluntly.

Mrs. Avery gave her a sharp look. "You don't know?"

Back to square one again. "No," she said. "I—"

"Milton," Mrs. Avery said sharply, narrowing her eyes at her husband. "Are you trying to scare this nice young girl?"

Maggie felt a trickle of sweat run down between her shoulder blades. So she was right all along. Something awful had happened in that house. She knew it! She wasn't crazy after all!

Maggie sat down at the table, trying to stay calm.

Mr. Avery set his cap down. "Such a sad story," he muttered.

"Please, Milton, we didn't even know the poor people—the Helfers," Mrs. Avery chimed in. She shuffled back to the stove to lift the whistling kettle. "So many horrible stories on this street . . ."

Mr. Avery continued. "There was a girl about your age—named Miranda. Pretty girl with blond hair."

Miranda!

Maggie knew instantly that Miranda had to be the blond girl in her dream!

"Did Miranda live in my house?" Maggie asked eagerly.

"She and her family lived in your house, yes," answered Mr. Avery.

"Milton, that's enough," Mrs. Avery spoke up.

"No, please tell me," Maggie pleaded.

"She was killed," the old woman blurted out. "Murdered."

"She was stabbed," Mr. Avery said in a hushed whisper. "Stabbed right in her own bed."

chapter

12

Justin had his arm around her. That felt good.

It was Saturday night. The movie he had taken her to was a goofball comedy. Maggie usually enjoyed silly movies, but this time she couldn't lose herself in the story.

A girl was murdered, really murdered, in my bed and now I'm dreaming about her. That was all Maggie could think about.

After the movie, Justin kept his arm around her as he guided her out with the crowd, out into the mall parking lot. It was a balmy spring night, the air soft and sweet. A pale half-moon floated low in a purple sky.

"I guess you didn't like the movie as much as I did," Justin said.

"No, I liked it," Maggie lied.

She suddenly had the feeling that she was being watched.

She turned and stepped out from under Justin's arm.

Dawn, her arm in a cast, was standing at the edge of the parking lot with Tiffany. She waved to Maggie. "Don't you want to sign my cast?"

"Dawn!" Maggie cried, startled to see her. "I've been trying to call you. I—hope you still don't think—" She hurried over to them. Justin followed slowly behind.

"Guess I should apologize," Dawn said, flashing her a warm smile. "I said some pretty weird things after I fell."

"Well, you have to believe me. I didn't do it, Dawn," Maggie said simply.

Dawn shrugged. "Well, somebody pushed me. But it doesn't really matter now." She grinned at Maggie. "Tiffany's going to beat you out for the two-hundred IM anyway. Hey, Justin."

Justin nodded. "Hey." Then he tugged on Maggie's arm, impatient to lead her away.

Maggie signed Dawn's cast.

"We've got to get going," Justin urged.

"See you at practice," Maggie told Tiffany. She told Dawn she'd call her. Then she hurried after Justin, who had already started toward his car.

Maggie couldn't help sneaking glances back at the two girls. Even though she knew she hadn't pushed Dawn, Maggie still felt guilty.

"I know Dawn thinks I pushed her," Maggie told Justin. "No matter what she says."

"That's Dawn for you," Justin said, unlocking the door on the passenger side for Maggie. "Like when she loses a meet, there's always an excuse." He opened the door for her. "And if she trips, she was pushed."

"I guess," Maggie replied thoughtfully. But as she climbed into the car, her good mood faded. The uneasy feeling had returned.

Justin's car was upholstered in soft black leather. Maggie settled back in her seat. Relax, she told herself.

Justin started the car, then fiddled with a control on the dash. The top cranked down, letting in the moonlight and the warm spring breezes. He smiled at her. Then he pulled out of the parking lot, making the tires squeal.

They didn't drive far. About a block from the mall, he parked on a deserted street.

Maggie glanced around, surprised. "Why are we stopping here?"

Justin pretended to peer outside. "Looks like we're lost," he said, and grinned. Even in the evening darkness, his blue eyes were gorgeous.

Maggie grinned back. "I don't mind."

Justin leaned over, slowly bringing his face toward hers.

Her eyes were locked on his. She felt her heart start to pound with excitement.

But she quickly found that kissing was awkward in the tiny car. For one thing it had bucket seats. They were so low, it was hard to reach each other.

Then they both got tangled in their seat belts.

Untwisting herself, a gruesome thought suddenly filled Maggie with cold dread.

This was what that girl had felt like when she got tangled in the covers. Miranda. The girl who died in Maggie's bed.

She was tangled, tangled in the bedsheets. And then she was stabbed.

With a sigh, Maggie clicked her seat belt open and let it slide away from her shoulders.

Why can't I stop thinking about Miranda?

Justin reached for her.

"Wait," Maggie said, pulling her face away.

"Huh? What's wrong?"

She didn't want to tell him. "Nothing," she said. "It's just—so cramped in here."

Justin uttered an annoyed sigh. He sat back in his seat and stared straight ahead in angry silence. Finally he turned back to her. "There's a nice big tree over there," he said. "We could sit under it."

She hesitated. "I'm really sorry. My mind—It's somewhere else."

Justin sighed again. "Mags, what's wrong?" he asked finally. "All of a sudden—"

"It's that dream again," she confessed.

"The dream?" Justin's face knotted in confusion. "What dream?"

"Remember I told you about a nightmare I had? A girl with blond hair, I couldn't see her face . . ."

Justin's face remained blank.

"I tried to put it out of my mind," Maggie rushed on. "But then I had the dream again, and this time the girl was stabbed, in my bed."

"In your dream," Justin corrected her.

"Right," said Maggie. "That's what I thought. It was just a dream. But guess what I found out from my neighbors? The last people who lived in our house—their daughter was murdered. In bed. In *my* bed."

"Weird," Justin muttered. "Who was she?"

"Her name was Miranda Helfer. Did you know her? Did you ever hear about the murder?"

"Miranda Helfer?" He thought for a moment. "No. Never heard of her."

Justin's expression brightened. "Well, that explains why you're having nightmares."

"No. Don't you see?" Maggie said impatiently. "I had the nightmares *before* I knew about the dead girl."

"Huh?" Justin reacted with surprise.

"The real estate guy didn't tell us," Maggie continued. "And I started dreaming about the murder my first night in that old canopy bed. There's no way I could have known about it, Justin. No way. So it must be something—you know—supernatural."

Justin narrowed his eyes. "What do you mean?"

"You know, like the bed remembers the murder and it's trying to transmit it to me, to warn me, to—*something!*"

Justin ran his hand through his dark, wavy hair. "Mags," he said, rolling his eyes scornfully. "The *bed* remembers? The *bed*? Earth calling Maggie. Earth calling Maggie . . ."

"I know, I know. It sounds dumb. But can you

think of a better explanation?" Maggie demanded earnestly. "Why am I having this dream?"

"Maggie," Justin said, sounding more than a little annoyed. "Dreams are always mixed up and crazy."

"Well, I think this one means something," Maggie replied heatedly. "I think Miranda is trying to tell me something. I think she's trying to warn me about something."

Justin gaped at her. He let out a high-pitched giggle. "From the grave?"

Maggie nodded solemnly. "From the grave."

Maggie cupped her hand at the perfect angle, cutting deep into the water with each stroke. She was swimming beautifully. She could feel it.

She wasn't surprised when she pulled her head up at the end of the race and saw she had finished first—by half a lap.

Behind her, the water churned. The other two swimmers, Andrea and Tiffany, swam neck and neck, battling it out for second.

Hanging on to the edge of the pool, Maggie started shouting, "Go, Andrea! Pull!"

With her bathing cap and dark goggles, Andrea looked like some strange water creature surging through the pool. Maggie barely recognized her. "You can do it, Andrea!" she shouted.

But Tiffany pulled ahead, and her hand hit the wall first.

"Okay, good race," Coach Randall called out a moment later. "I need to see the three of you over here."

They stood in a semicircle around the team bench, where Coach Randall sat, studying the notes on her clipboard. Even though it was warm in the pool area, the three girls all held their hands crossed over the chests of their dripping bathing suits, as if to protect themselves.

Maggie had always noticed that about swimming. You felt vulnerable when you came out of the water.

Raising her eyes to the bleachers, Maggie spotted Dawn in the top row. She was dressed in street clothes, her feet on the bench below her. Even at this distance, Maggie could see that Dawn wasn't smiling.

Well, what did I expect? Maggie asked herself. If I had broken my arm and lost out on swimming All-State, I wouldn't be in the friendliest mood either.

Coach Randall scribbled something on her clipboard. "All right," she announced. "Maggie, Tiffany, you're going to swim the two-hundred IM in the All-State."

Tiffany danced away from them, throwing her arms up in the air excitedly. "I made it!" she shouted to Dawn.

Dawn cheered. "Way to go, Tiffany!" She didn't congratulate Maggie, of course—no surprise there.

Maggie congratulated Tiffany. But her smile faded fast when she caught Andrea's expression.

Andrea's lower jaw was jutting out in an expression Maggie knew only too well. Her sister was fuming.

"Andrea," the coach continued, "if it's any consolation, you didn't miss out by much. You're swimming better than you ever have."

"Great," Andrea muttered.

"I want you to keep training hard, Andrea," Coach Randall instructed. "The two-hundred IM is the most important event. You're our number-one alternate."

"Obviously," grumbled Andrea, rolling her eyes. "There's no one else left."

Coach Randall stared at her sternly. "There's a whole team left. There are eleven other girls. If you don't want to swim the two-hundred IM, just say so."

Andrea shrugged.

"Being an alternate is important," Coach Randall continued. "And don't forget that you're a year younger than Maggie and Tiffany. You've got another year to go."

Maggie gave Andrea a sympathetic glance.

"You can stop with the pity act!" Andrea snapped at her. She turned sharply and stalked off to the showers.

Coach Randall turned to Maggie. "Don't worry," she said. "She'll get over it."

Somehow, I doubt that, thought Maggie.

It wasn't the first time she wished that her younger sister didn't hate her so much.

Maggie couldn't get comfortable. The sheets felt as if they were burning.

Normally she liked to sleep on her right side. But

that night, she could hear—and feel—her heart pounding. It made her so uncomfortable. As if any moment her heart might stop.

Tossing and turning.

She was tossing and turning.

Just like the girl in the dream.

No. Please no.

I'm tossing and turning like Miranda.

I'm just like Miranda.

She felt herself falling now, falling into the dream.

No turning back.

She fell through a pink haze.

From high above, she gazed down at the billowing pink canopy of her bed.

I'm dreaming, she told herself. It's just a dream.

Why didn't that thought offer any comfort?

Through the pink canopy. Through the pink gauzy top. Into the bed.

And she saw the girl. She saw Miranda. Her ash-blond hair matted and wet against the pillow.

The girl's face was turned away as always.

Then the dark shadow swept over the bed.

Maggie whirled. Just in time to see the glint of the knife blade in the dim light.

"No!" Maggie screamed.

The scream must have been loud enough to wake her up.

She found herself wide awake, sitting up in bed.

Her eyes darted around the dark bedroom.

I don't want to wake up now! she told herself.

I want to finish the dream. I want to see more.

I *need* to see more!

She settled back against the pillow, determined to go back to sleep and finish the dream.

But lying in the dark, staring up at the canopy fluttering in the gentle breeze from the open window, Maggie suddenly knew she wasn't alone.

It's not a dream, she knew.

It's real. Not a dream. And someone else is in my bedroom.

The figure stood in the dark corner of the room, just where the attacker always hid in her dream.

With a shudder of terror, Maggie pulled herself up—and saw who it was.

Andrea!

"Andrea? Andrea? It's you?"

Andrea crossed the room quickly to Maggie's bed.

And as Andrea moved toward her, Maggie saw something gleam in her sister's hand. She recognized the silver glint of the knife.

chapter

13

"Andrea—what do you want? What are you doing in here?" Maggie whispered.

"I couldn't sleep," came the whispered reply. "I was trying out some new hairstyles. I just came in to borrow your curling iron."

She held it up. The glint of light, Maggie now realized, was the silvery rod of the curling iron.

"Sorry I woke you," Andrea whispered. She tiptoed out of the room. "Do you want the door open?"

Maggie was breathing too hard to answer.

"I'll shut it partway," Andrea said.

After Andrea left, Maggie remained still, staring at the doorway, waiting for her breathing to return to normal.

Andrea crossing the room in the dark. The metallic shimmer of the knife. That was from my dream, she thought.

But how could that be?

Am I really cracking up?

She didn't have long to think about it.

Suddenly the door to her room creaked open.

She heard the thud of soft footsteps. But she couldn't see anyone!

Without warning, Gus's head popped up on the side of the bed, his dark, sad eyes staring at her in the dark. Maggie was so glad to see him, she flung her arms around his neck and kissed him on the nose.

Gus licked her ear. Then he trotted back out the door again. She heard him thump-thumping down the front steps.

"Be sure to get lots of rest." Maggie suddenly remembered the coach's instructions. She closed her eyes.

I've got to sleep. Got to sleep . . .

She lay still. It seemed like an eternity—probably only about five minutes. She opened her eyes. This was pointless. She had never been so wide awake in her life.

Okay, Dad, she said to herself. Time to take your advice. Her father had always said that if you couldn't sleep, get out of bed and read until you were sleepy.

She swung her legs out of the bed. The floor felt refreshingly cool. She crossed to her bookshelf and searched for something boring to read. *Moby Dick.* That ought to do the trick. Dad always said it was the most boring great book ever written.

She remembered another piece of advice from her dad on insomnia. He said it helped to leave the bedroom until you felt sleepy.

Mr. Travers had been a real expert on insomnia because he suffered from it. Many late nights, when Maggie would wander downstairs, she'd find him sitting in the kitchen, drinking his favorite remedy—a tall mug of hot cocoa—and reading.

Moby Dick weighed a ton. Carrying the heavy hardback under one arm, she padded out into the hall. Through the crack under Andrea's door she could see her sister's light still on. She didn't move toward it, but headed through the hall and down the front stairs.

Gus was sleeping by the footstool in the living room, snoring like crazy. No insomnia problem there.

The empty kitchen was as silent as a grave. She opened the fridge, letting the cool air spill out onto her bare legs.

Somewhere in the house, a floorboard creaked.

She listened, her body instantly tense. Usually, when the house made noises, she told herself it was Gus. But Gus was in the living room, sleeping.

It's just the house settling, she assured herself.

Outside, the wind made a shutter bang.

There was nothing in the fridge she wanted, but she kept the door open anyway, just for the light.

She stood still and listened a moment more. All quiet now. She closed the fridge.

She flicked on the light and sat down at the kitchen table. She didn't even open the novel. There was no way she could concentrate on a whaling story.

Could I get back to the dream? she wondered.

Could I close my eyes and drift back into it? Could I finally see the girl's face, see the attacker? Could I finish it once and for all?

She surprised herself by her eagerness to get to the end of it.

Am I tired enough to sleep now? She closed her eyes. She could feel her exhaustion, just under the surface.

She turned off the kitchen light and climbed the front stairs. She had been in the house for only two weeks, but already she could find her way around in the dark. It had become a little familiar.

Maybe someday it would seem like home.

Back in her room she stopped short. The blankets on the bed had been pulled up.

Strange. Maggie was sure she had left them crumpled up at the foot of the bed, where she had kicked them off.

She crossed to the bed and reached for the covers.

She yanked them down—

And screamed when she saw the knife, its long blade plunged deep into her pillow.

chapter
14

With a shudder, Maggie raised her hands to her face and backed away from the bed.

When she reached the open doorway, she turned and ran.

She felt sick. Her stomach heaved. The blood throbbed at her temples.

Andrea! It had to be Andrea.

Maggie remembered the crack of light under Andrea's door. Andrea was still awake.

Was the dream warning me about Andrea? Maggie asked herself, fighting back her terror, her anger.

Does Andrea hate me *that* much?

At the end of the hall, in the darkness, her mother's door flew open. Mrs. Travers came running out in her nightgown. Maggie lurched toward her.

"Mom—Mom!" She grabbed her mother by the hand and pulled her back into her mother's bedroom.

Mrs. Travers's eyes went wide with worry. "What? What is it, Maggie! What's wrong?"

"Andrea—" Maggie choked out.

"What? What *about* Andrea?"

"The kn-knife."

"What knife? What, Maggie? Is Andrea okay?"

"Me! Me!" Maggie screamed frantically.

Clutching both of her mother's hands, she tugged her back down the hall. "Andrea put the knife in my bed!" she cried hoarsely.

"What are you talking about?"

Maggie pushed her mother into her bedroom. "There!" she cried, pointing at her bed.

Mrs. Travers clicked on the ceiling light.

They both stared at Maggie's bed.

The covers were down, just as she had left them.

But the pillowcase was smooth and uncut.

And the knife was gone.

chapter

15

"*I*'m not crazy!" Maggie shrieked.

Mrs. Travers drew back, tugging tensely at a tangle of hair, her eyes narrowed at Maggie, studying Maggie.

"I'm not crazy, Mom!" Maggie insisted in a shrill shriek of a voice.

With a furious cry, she pushed past her mother and ran out the door.

And down the hall.

"Don't wake Andrea up!" Mrs. Travers called behind her.

But Maggie shoved her sister's door open and snapped on the light.

Andrea lay facedown on the bed, the covers pulled up over her shoulders.

"Quit acting!" Maggie shrieked. "You're up! I know you're up!"

Andrea groaned and turned over slowly, shielding her eyes. "Wha—?"

Mrs. Travers stormed into the room. "Maggie, leave your sister alone. I'm serious."

"Leave *her* alone?" Maggie laughed wildly. "Leave *her* alone? She stabbed a knife into my bed, Mother! She—she—she's trying to drive me crazy!"

Maggie's whole body trembled in rage. She lunged forward, grabbed Andrea's shoulders, started to shake them hard.

"Where's the knife, Andrea? Where? Where'd you hide it? Under here?" She let go of Andrea and jerked her pillow off the bed.

"Let go!" Andrea cried sleepily. "What is your problem, Maggie?"

Mrs. Travers grabbed Maggie's shoulders and tried to pull her away from Andrea's bed.

But Maggie whirled around. "Her light was on until two seconds ago!" she cried. "Her light was on. She wasn't asleep, Mom! She's faking! She stuck the knife in my pillow! I swear to you!"

"What knife?" Andrea demanded, pulling her pillow out of Maggie's arms. "Where would I get a knife?" She turned to her mother. "What is Maggie talking about?"

"I'm not sure," Mrs. Travers replied wearily. "Come with me, Maggie," she said softly. "Let's talk about it in the morning, okay? When you've calmed down a little."

"I'll *never* calm down!" Maggie insisted. But she allowed her mother to lead her out of the room.

"You're crazy, Maggie," she heard Andrea mutter from her bed. "You're totally crazy."

The whistle blew shrilly. Coach Randall stared down at her watch. "All right, girls, listen up."

Tuesday afternoon, the end of another long practice. Maggie was clinging to the pool edge, beside her teammates, listening to the coach. She glanced up at Dawn, watching from her usual perch at the top of the bleachers.

Coach Randall paced up and down at the pool's edge. "As you know," Coach Randall went on, "Friday is the All-State meet, so for those of you who'll be competing, there isn't much time left to get you in tip-top shape. What do you say, everybody? Five more laps?"

There were groans all down the pool. Coach Randall's face twisted into an expression of mock surprise. "Oh, you're disappointed we're doing only five? You're right. We'll make it ten."

More groans. But Coach Randall clapped her hands. "No fooling. Everyone on the diving blocks. Five laps, freestyle. Maggie—Tiffany—let's see why you guys are swimming the two-hundred IM for us."

Maggie took the lane between Andrea and Tiffany.

"You're going to lose," Andrea muttered under her breath as she pulled down her goggles.

"Thanks for the vote of confidence," Maggie said with a bitter smile. She crouched into her diving stance. Andrea had done her a favor. Andrea's remark reminded Maggie of how much she hated losing.

The whistle blew and Maggie pushed off hard, heading straight off into the cold blue water.

She started strong, but almost immediately her energy flagged. Her body remembered how tired she was, even if her mind had forgotten. Every time she turned her head to breathe, she saw Tiffany match her stroke for stroke.

Maggie stroked harder, faster. But when she turned her head to breathe now, she saw Tiffany's midsection. She was falling behind!

One lap, that's all it was. But it seemed like a mile. Her hand smacked the floats that marked the lane. Stinging pain ran up her arm.

She realized she was veering too close to Andrea. She tried to straighten out, but it cost her more time.

Maggie had already lost once to Tiffany this week. That had been painful enough. But lose to Andrea? She had never lost to her sister in her life.

With a low groan, Maggie picked up the pace, punishing her exhausted muscles.

Tiffany finished first. Maggie and Andrea swam neck and neck.

Maggie could hear Andrea groaning in anger and frustration.

Maggie let out a growl and stretched with every muscle for the wall.

Her fingertips touched the wall.

Then Andrea touched.

Maggie gasped loudly, struggling to catch her breath.

She shook water from her ears, listening as Coach

Randall called off the top three finishers. Tiffany. Maggie. Andrea.

Without turning her head, Maggie could feel Andrea slump against the wall. Then Coach Randall blew her whistle again and ordered everyone to hit the showers.

It took Maggie a few minutes to feel strong enough to drag herself out of the pool. She was the last one out.

"You looked like you were struggling out there," Coach Randall told her, frowning.

"Did I?" Maggie asked.

"Be sure to get plenty of rest from now till Friday," the coach told her, slapping her on the back.

Sure thing. Get a lot of rest. Easy to say. Somehow, Maggie doubted that Coach Randall had nightmares about a girl getting stabbed, or found a knife plunged into her pillow.

She trudged into the locker room and wearily dropped down onto the bench in front of her locker. Most of the team were already in the showers, their shouts and laughter spilling out into the dressing area.

A locker door slammed. Maggie knew it was Andrea. Hiding her feelings had never been one of Andrea's strengths.

"Beat you again," Tiffany called to Maggie. "That's twice in a row. You're slipping, Travers." Tiffany stood a few lockers down, buttoning up her blouse.

Maggie nodded. "Yeah. Well . . ." She turned to Andrea. "Good race."

Andrea was bent over, struggling to untie a knot in her sneaker laces. She heaved the sneaker down hard in frustration. "Please! Just leave me alone," she muttered.

Fully dressed, Tiffany came over and sat down next to Maggie. She's being awfully friendly, Maggie thought. She had never seen Tiffany so happy before.

"How do you think we'll do on Friday?" Tiffany asked.

"We'll kill them," Maggie promised.

"Wouldn't that be awesome?" Tiffany asked. "To win at All-State?"

"Awesome," Maggie repeated without enthusiasm. She caught the scowl on Andrea's face.

"See you," Tiffany said, climbing to her feet. "Just three days to go." She hoisted her gym bag onto her shoulder and started out through the pool exit.

"Maggie?" It was Coach Randall in the doorway of her office. "Can I see you a second?"

"Uh-oh," Andrea whispered. "Maggie's in trouble."

"Grow up," Maggie told her sharply. She draped a towel around herself, hooking it tightly above her chest.

Coach Randall was sitting behind her desk when Maggie came in. The coach smiled warmly. "How are you feeling?"

"Exhausted and excited at the same time," Maggie replied.

Coach Randall nodded. "Your backstroke was looking better today. A lot less side-to-side movement."

"Yeah, it felt good," Maggie said. What does she want? Maggie wondered. Since when does she like to chat?

"So how's everything else?" the coach asked casually.

"Everything else?"

"You know," Coach Randall replied. "Life, things at home, boyfriends, that kind of thing."

Whoa, thought Maggie. What's up with Coach Randall? Why is she asking me all this?

What was she supposed to do? Pour her heart out? My father died, my boyfriend has been ignoring me ever since I told him about my weird nightmare, I found a knife in my pillow, and I think my bed is haunted.

No, that wouldn't sound too good.

"Everything's fine," Maggie said.

Coach Randall stared at her for a long time, studying Maggie's eyes. "I've been a little worried about you lately, Maggie. You haven't been yourself."

"I'm fine," Maggie insisted. "Really."

"I hope you and Andrea have worked things out," the coach said, leaning over her cluttered desk.

"Yeah. No problem," Maggie lied.

They talked for a little while longer. Finally Coach Randall repeated her instructions about getting plenty of rest, and let her go.

As she left the office, Maggie passed the wide-open door to the pool and glanced in.

What *was* that?

"Oh!" She gasped, not believing her eyes.

She started through the doorway.

Then stopped.

She cried out in horror as she saw Tiffany lying facedown on the floor, bright red blood puddling around her on the tiles.

chapter

16

"*T*iffany!" Maggie screamed.

Tiffany didn't stir.

Maggie bent over her.

And saw the blood-spotted knife.

And then the stab wound in Tiffany's side.

"Oh oh ohh . . ." Maggie uttered a shocked groan and picked up the knife—

Just as Coach Randall came running in from the locker room, and two other teachers pushed through the front doors to the pool.

Maggie glanced up, frozen in horror. Her hand was covered in warm, sticky blood. The knife fell from her hand.

The teachers, their faces wide with horror, were running toward her.

Maggie jumped to her feet. "I didn't do it!" she cried. "Really! I didn't do it!"

* * *

Maggie lay on the living room sofa, staring up at the ceiling.

"No one really suspected you, sweetie," Mrs. Travers said. She sat by Maggie's feet. "Why would they? You had no reason to stab Tiffany. As if you would ever do such a thing even if you *had* a reason!"

"The police—they asked so many questions," Maggie moaned.

"They were just doing their jobs," her mother replied. "But they never thought you stabbed Tiffany."

"I'm just glad she's going to be okay," Maggie said, sighing.

"Her mother says she's in pain, but she'll be okay," Mrs. Travers said. She chewed her bottom lip. "Too bad Tiffany didn't see who attacked her. She told the doctors someone grabbed her from behind."

Maggie felt something wet and warm slop against her hand. She lowered her eyes to find Gus licking her hand as it dangled off the sofa. He panted up at her, putting a paw up on her arm.

"Good dog," she said, stroking his head. "Good sweet dog." That was one of the great things about dogs. They always loved you no matter what was going on.

Andrea was in the kitchen, talking to Tiffany on the phone. Maggie could hear snatches of Andrea's end of the conversation. "Important that you rest . . . Plenty of other meets . . . Thank goodness you're okay . . . Could have been so much worse."

Well, thought Maggie, at least Tiffany is going to be okay. But there was no way Tiffany could swim Friday.

First Dawn, then Tiffany.

Now there were only two swimmers left. Maggie and—

Maggie sat up as Andrea entered the room. Andrea had a pleased smile on her face. She couldn't hide her happiness.

Andrea was in the meet now, Maggie realized. She'd swim the two-hundred IM in Tiffany's place.

"Tiffany's going to be fine," Andrea assured Maggie and her mother. As if *that* were what she was smiling about! Maggie thought bitterly.

"That's wonderful, Andrea," Mrs. Travers said. "You see, Maggie? Everything's going to be okay." She stood up. "I'd better start dinner. How do hot dogs and baked beans sound?"

Mom must really be worried about me, thought Maggie. The last time she let us eat hot dogs was the week after Dad's funeral.

Maggie and Andrea had done the cooking that week. They made franks and beans every night until there were no franks left in the freezer.

"You know what this means, don't you, Mags?" Andrea asked. "It means I go to All-State."

Maggie nodded, but she wasn't really paying attention. She was distracted by a very disturbing thought.

Tiffany was stabbed. The girl in my dream was stabbed.

Is there a connection?

Crazy thoughts, Maggie told herself. Crazy thoughts.

But she couldn't force the idea away.

Andrea began pacing in front of her, her hands shoved deep into the front pockets of her denim cutoffs. "I can't believe it. How many people will be there Friday, do you think? I'm so nervous. I know I'll faint or puke or something. Has anyone ever puked in the pool during a meet?"

"Tiffany was stabbed," Maggie murmured, not really hearing her sister. "Was the dream trying to warn me—!"

"Oh, please don't start with that dream stuff again!" Andrea begged. "You're just making yourself crazy, Maggie."

She started pacing again. "I'm better than Tiffany anyway. So I guess it's lucky in a way, what happened."

"Lucky?" Andrea's words broke into Maggie's troubled thoughts. Her mouth dropped open. "Lucky that Tiffany got stabbed?"

"I know. It sounds awful," Andrea replied without any emotion. "But what am I supposed to do? Act depressed about making the team?"

Maggie jumped up. She was so furious at Andrea, she could barely speak. "The way you're talking, people might think *you* stabbed Tiffany!" Maggie sputtered.

Andrea laughed scornfully. "What an idea!" she exclaimed. "What an idea!"

* * *

"Please—please help me!"

Maggie tossed on the bed, back in the nightmare. Only the dream had changed.

The girl with the ash-blond hair was no longer sleeping in the bed.

Now the girl was running, running for her life.

And Maggie was running with her.

"Miranda!" Maggie called to her. "Miranda—wait for me!"

She followed Miranda through a long, dark tunnel. The tunnel walls were wet and slimy. The roof of the tunnel was low, so that Miranda and Maggie had to bend their heads.

Miranda kept slipping and falling over loose rocks on the floor. Every time she fell, she hurried to her feet again and rushed forward.

Maggie followed her. She knew it was a dream. But it was as real as life to her. "Miranda! Miranda!" she called.

If only the girl in the dream could hear her!

The dark tunnel became narrower and narrower, as if the rock walls were slowly closing in.

Miranda kept running. The tunnel twisted and turned.

Maggie could see only the girl's back, her hair bobbing up and down as she ran.

"Let me see your face! Miranda—please let me see your face!"

But she didn't have to see Miranda's face to know that she was desperate, terrified.

All at once Maggie realized why.

Someone was pursuing Miranda through the tunnel, pursuing her with a knife.

Closer. Closer.

The knife blade gleamed in the gray tunnel light.

Maggie gasped as Miranda slipped and fell once again.

Maggie fell with her this time. Fell through an endless, swirling pink haze.

Below her, the pink canopy came into view.

Maggie's heart froze. She was heading for the canopy.

Miranda was back in the bed now, her head turned away.

So the tunnel was the *beginning* of the nightmare! Maggie realized.

All the other times, I came into the dream in the middle!

The dream repeated as before.

But this time, slowly, very slowly, the girl turned over.

And finally Maggie saw her face.

A pretty face. A terrified face.

And as Maggie stared at the face, she saw the hand of the attacker.

The dark figure moved forward to stab Miranda.

Then Maggie woke up.

Wide awake.

Her eyes blinked open. Her heart thudding.

She took a deep breath, then another.

I'm awake. I'm okay. I saw her face.

And now I'm awake.

Maggie didn't have a chance to scream before the cold hand clamped tightly over her mouth.

This isn't the dream! she realized. This is happening now—to me!

Andrea?

Was it Andrea again?

No.

As the cold hand pressed down over her mouth, Maggie stared up into the darkness.

And saw Miranda.

No! It can't be!

Maggie raised both hands to shove the hand away.

Miranda glared down at her, pale hair falling wildly over her forehead.

"Are you—a *ghost?*" Maggie managed to utter in a choked whisper.

Miranda nodded.

"You—you're really a ghost?"

Miranda nodded again and raised the knife.

chapter

17

*T*he knife blade shone in the dim light from the window.

Maggie squirmed desperately and rolled to the floor. She landed hard. Pain shot up through her body.

"Miranda—no!" she pleaded.

The ghost glared down at her, dark eyes peering through tangles of hair that tumbled over her face.

The knife bright in her hand.

"Miranda—please!"

"Maggie?" Mrs. Travers's worried voice rang out in the hall. Maggie heard her mother's footsteps rapidly approaching.

The ghost took a silent step back.

"Maggie—are you okay?" Mrs. Travers called.

Maggie watched in dazed horror as Miranda yanked open the bedroom window—and disappeared.

Maggie pulled herself up from the floor. Her body convulsed in a single shudder of terror.

The bedroom door flew open. The light clicked on. "Maggie—" Mrs. Travers stopped, seeing the dazed expression on Maggie's face.

"Mom—the ghost!" Maggie cried.

"Huh?"

"The ghost! The girl in the dream—she was here! Quick—look!"

She grabbed her mother and pulled her to the window. "Look, Mom! The girl—"

Mrs. Travers leaned out the open window. The wind ruffled her nightgown. A few seconds later, she pulled back into the room.

"There's no one out there, Maggie." Her expression was grim.

"Mom—she was here in my room! She floated out the window. She—she had a knife and—"

Mrs. Travers uttered a low cry, moved forward quickly, and wrapped Maggie in her arms. "Oh, Maggie," she cried in a trembling voice. "Don't worry. I'll get you help. I'll get you help right away, dear. We'll find a good doctor. You'll be okay. I know you will."

"Now, in your projects next week, you're going to be growing your very own versions of stalactites and stalagmites," Mrs. Harrison told them. She shone her flashlight up at the roof of the cave, where the pointy formations hung straight down like daggers.

"They look like icicles," said Carly Pedersen, her voice echoing in the cavern.

"Exactly right," Mrs. Harrison agreed. "And they're formed the same way, but much more slowly. In fact, the word *stalactite* comes from the Greek word for dripping."

Wednesday afternoon. Outside, it was cold and dark and cloudy—more like a winter day than a spring one. And that was *outside*. In the cave the temperature was at least ten degrees colder.

Maggie wrapped her arms around herself. Why hadn't she brought a jacket as the rest of the kids had? Probably because she couldn't think sensibly. All she could think about was that she had seen a dead girl, a ghost. And that the ghost had tried to stab her.

Maggie searched for Dawn in the crowd of students clustered around Mrs. Harrison. She found Dawn staring at her and glowering.

Now what have I done? Maggie asked herself. What is Dawn's problem?

"All right," Mrs. Harrison said. "As you can see, there are three different tunnels leading back from the mouth of the cave. Don't worry, they all connect up eventually. But it's a real maze back there, so stick together. Okay, let's split up into our groups of four, find your way through, and then we'll meet outside in half an hour."

Groups of four? Maggie glanced around in a sudden panic.

When were the groups assigned? Must have been Friday.

"You're with us," Deena Martinson told her.

"Oh, thanks," Maggie said, relieved.

"This way," Deena called, leading her into the blackness that was the back of the huge cavern. Maggie followed obediently.

Up ahead, another member of their group, Deena's friend Jade Smith was exclaiming, "Wow! The walls are so slimy!"

Maggie had to stoop to keep her head from brushing the rough, wet ceiling of the tunnel.

The parks department had put in some lights to help guide the way. And the rest of her group had flashlights. Another thing Maggie had forgotten.

But even with flashlights, it was still gloomy. And getting colder and colder the farther back they went.

"Remind me never to become a geologist," Maggie murmured.

"I hope there are no bats," Deena said.

Finally the tunnel opened into a wider space. Maggie held back. What was that fluttering sound?

"Bats are supposed to be good," Jade whispered.

"Has anyone told the bats?" Deena replied.

"Look!" Deena pointed. "A whole mess of tunnels leading off this one."

Maggie slipped and almost fell. She suddenly felt dizzy. She leaned against the wall for a moment, holding her head down until the feeling passed.

When she raised her eyes, she saw that the cavern was empty. Her group had taken off without her.

Hearing them up ahead, she plunged into the mouth of the nearest tunnel.

She moved as fast as she could, crouching low and picking her way over the loose rocks. The tunnel kept branching off, and she tried to follow the voices of her group.

But soon Maggie realized that she was no longer hearing any voices up ahead. And she couldn't hear any voices behind her either.

She stared into the darkness of the narrow tunnel.

Okay, Maggie, she told herself, stay calm.

Just follow the tunnel. You'll come out somewhere and—

"Oh!" She gasped as she thought she saw the tunnel walls begin to close in.

"No!"

Just like in the dream.

Miranda in the dark tunnel. Running. Running.

No. No. This isn't the dream.

The dream isn't coming true, she assured herself.

Take a deep breath. Then simply head back the way you came.

But which way was that?

She'd lost her sense of direction.

Which way? Which way? Which way?

She couldn't see a thing, surrounded by heavy darkness.

Then she heard footsteps. Behind her.

Maggie took a few steps toward them. Then she stopped.

The footsteps kept coming.
This isn't the dream, she told herself.
This isn't the dream.
The footsteps moved closer. Closer.
"Who—who is it?" Maggie called in a trembling
voice.

chapter
18

No answer.

Maggie could hear shallow breathing, the sound echoing off the narrow tunnel walls.

Closer.

"Who *is* it?" she repeated, her fear making her voice high and shrill.

Still no answer.

The breathing grew louder. The footsteps crunched over the rock floor. Closer. Closer.

Choked with terror, Maggie spun away from the sounds and forced herself to start jogging.

Over the pounding of her sneakers, she could hear her pursuer begin to run too.

She couldn't deny it anymore.

She was being chased!

Just like Miranda. Just like in the dream.

"Ow!" Maggie scraped her knee against something sticking out of the tunnel wall. The pain raced through her body, but she kept running.

Then before she even realized it, she was screaming for help. The sound just ripped out of her.

She ran through the darkness. The dream had become real. Her life had become the dream.

She didn't get far. She tripped over a rock and went down hard.

She could hear the footsteps padding closer.

As she scrambled back to her feet, her knees throbbed with pain.

She turned a corner and slammed into a wall. Her hand touched something wet and slimy.

And then she heard dry fluttering overhead, like hundreds of tiny umbrellas opening all at once.

Something brushed her face. Something furry. She screamed!

"Help me! Somebody—help me! Get me out! Out of here!"

The tunnel vibrated with the sound of a thousand flapping wings.

The footsteps crunched closer.

Screaming for help, Maggie ran into another cold, wet wall.

A dead end.

I'm trapped, she realized.

chapter

19

Maggie pressed her back up against the wall as if she could push her way through the rock.

The footsteps pounded closer.

Overcome with terror, she collapsed to her knees.

She listened hard, too frightened to move. Any second, she knew, her attacker would appear and the knife would come down out of the darkness.

Now!

Or—

Now!

But nothing happened.

Breathing hard, her side aching, she climbed back to her feet.

The dream is real, she thought again. And my life is the dream.

Then she heard the footsteps again, very close. She pressed back helplessly against the rock.

The footsteps stopped. A flash of light.

The knife?

No. A flashlight played over her face.

"Mags?" A boy's voice, unsteady, muffled in the heavy wet air.

The flashlight burned into her eyes.

"Hey, are you okay?"

She felt a strong hand grab her arm, pull her to her feet.

"Justin?"

"Maggie—why did you run?" he asked breathlessly, still holding her arm. "I came searching for you. I called your name."

"I didn't hear. I only heard your footsteps," Maggie said, still trembling.

"Everyone is outside, waiting at the bus," he told her. "You were missing, so . . ."

"I got lost," she told him, leaning against him.

"Yeah, well, everyone's real worried about you," Justin said. "Let's get out of here."

She held on to him as he led the way out of the tunnel. Maggie heard the flap of bats' wings. She held her breath and kept walking.

"I—I thought you were the killer," she blurted out.

"What killer?"

"From my dream."

She instantly regretted telling him. She could feel his muscles tighten.

His expression hardened. "Maggie, I hope you're not starting up with that dream stuff again," he murmured.

Maggie stopped near one of the lights mounted in

the slimy cavern wall. The eerie glow of the naked bulb made Justin's normally handsome face look like a skull. "Sorry," Maggie whispered.

They walked the rest of the way out of the cave in silence.

Maggie strode quickly down the sidewalk. She didn't really know why she was in such a hurry. There was no reason to rush home.

One day had passed. She hadn't seen the ghost again, hadn't dreamed the dream. But the fear was always with her, there in the creepy old house, there at night in the canopy bed. She didn't want to talk to anyone, see anyone.

"Maggie!" someone called behind her.

She picked up her pace, pretending she hadn't heard.

"Hey, Mags! Slow down!" Justin appeared at her side, jogging to keep up. "Slow down! What's up?"

Why was he pretending everything was okay between them? He hadn't said a word to her since the day before in the cave.

"Nothing's up," she muttered, walking fast.

"Are you okay?" he asked.

"You mean, am I crazy?" she asked sharply.

He reacted as if he were stung. He grabbed her shoulder and made her stop. "I saw you weren't in school this morning. So I was worried."

"I had a doctor's appointment," Maggie said.

"A doctor's appointment? You sick?"

"Sick in the head," she muttered bitterly.

"You saw a shrink?"

She nodded.

Dr. Brenda Marsh was a soft-spoken, fortyish psychiatrist whom Mrs. Travers had seen a couple of times after her husband died. Mrs. Travers reported that she had been very helpful. But as far as Maggie and Andrea could tell, all she had done was tell their mother it was natural to feel depressed, and given her a mild sedative to help her sleep.

Maggie was surprised at how good it felt to talk to her. Brenda had an easy smile and kind eyes. She didn't seem shocked by anything Maggie said. Even when Maggie said she thought the dead girl, Miranda, was after her for revenge.

"I know it sounds crazy," Maggie had blurted out near the end of the session, "but I think it's because Miranda died. Now she wants me to die too."

"Dreams can be very upsetting," Dr. Marsh said softly. "They're also important clues to what's really bothering us. I want you to come in again and talk to me next week, all right?"

Maggie had nodded. "Sure, I'll come back."

"Did this shrink figure out what's going on with you?" Justin asked as they passed The Corner, a school hangout already filled with Shadyside kids.

Maggie shook her head. "She thinks the dreams are about something else, something that's bothering me."

"Oh," Justin said.

Maggie could tell the subject made Justin very uncomfortable. She knew it was coming between them. "Am I ever going to see you again?" she demanded.

He didn't hesitate. "How about tomorrow night?" He grinned at her, moving close. "First you win the two-hundred. Then you and I celebrate."

"First I have to win," Maggie said, frowning.

"You'll win," he told her. "I know it." He put his arms around her waist and hugged her.

It felt great, being in his arms again. She rested her head against his shoulder. For a moment, she forgot her troubles.

For a moment, it seemed as if nothing could harm her.

A very brief moment.

Then, gazing over Justin's shoulder, something caught her eye.

Standing across the street. On the sidewalk in front of the hedge. Miranda.

Miranda. The ghost. Standing there. Watching them.

Justin must have felt her body tense up, because he let go of her.

Maggie couldn't decide what to do. She wanted to cry out, to show Justin that Miranda really existed.

She wanted to run after Miranda. To grab her. To hold on to her. To show everyone she wasn't crazy.

But what would happen if she told Justin?

One more "crazy" episode—and Justin would give up on her.

She stared at the ghost with the pale blond hair shimmering in the afternoon sunlight.

She had to tell Justin. She had to show him.

"Justin!" Maggie cried. "Look! Across the street! It's her! It's the ghost! The girl from my dream! Look!"

"Huh?" Justin spun around, following her gaze to the hedge across the street.

There was no one there.

chapter

20

Maggie cried out in frustration and darted across the street.

No sign of Miranda.

She searched behind the hedge. She ran halfway down the next block.

Miranda had vanished. Vanished like a ghost.

"Maggie!" Justin chased after her, his features rigid.

"Later!" she called, waving him away. She didn't want to deal with him right then. She couldn't. She just couldn't.

She couldn't stand being with another person who thought she was crazy. And no matter what Justin said, she knew he'd be thinking it.

She wandered around the neighborhood near school, her head down, barely glancing up to check for traffic when she crossed streets. Every few blocks she would raise her head, expecting to see the ghost.

But no Miranda.

Wandering aimlessly, Maggie didn't get home until after five. As she walked into the living room, Andrea stepped out of the kitchen, carrying a tray of sizzling french fries.

"Hey, Maggie!" she called casually. Andrea was wearing her short-short khakis, an orange tank top, and gold hoop earrings. Maggie's gold hoop earrings.

"I hope you don't mind," Andrea said, cheerfully tilting her head from side to side to make the earrings bounce. "I was feeling like dressing up a little."

Maggie was in no mood to fight with her. "Where's Mom?" she asked dully.

"Out back. The Averys invited us to a cookout."

"Great," Maggie muttered without enthusiasm.

Dropping her backpack on the hall table, she followed Andrea into the backyard. Just beyond the hedge, she saw a familiar orange cap. Mr. Avery was standing over his barbecue grill, expertly flipping burgers with a metal spatula. When he saw her, he waved the spatula.

Gus was on a long leash tied to one of the Averys' birch trees. The dog started barking excitedly when he spotted Maggie.

Glass of iced tea in hand, a floppy straw hat on her head, Mrs. Travers stood talking with Mrs. Avery.

She draped an arm over Maggie when Maggie came up beside her. Mrs. Travers squeezed her shoulder. "Your ears must have been burning," her mother said, "with all the nice things Mrs. Avery has been saying about you."

Mrs. Avery beamed.

"Leave it to you," Mrs. Travers went on, "to introduce us to our new neighbors. Maggie has always been the friendly one in the family," she told her neighbor. "I don't know where she gets it from. It takes me so long to make friends. . . ." She trailed off.

Maggie could see from her eyes that she was thinking about their dad.

Andrea and Mr. Avery burst out laughing. Maggie watched them. They looked as if they had already become fast friends. "Dinner's ready," Mr. Avery called, handing a platter of burgers to Andrea.

"This is fine for me," Andrea joked as she hoisted the heavy platter, "but what will everyone else eat?"

Everyone laughed but Maggie.

They found places around the wooden picnic table set up in the backyard and began to dig in. Mrs. Avery had set out a large pitcher of pink lemonade that looked inviting, but it was too sour. She had obviously forgotten the sugar.

Andrea carried the conversation, chattering away gaily about school, the next day's swim meet, movies she wanted to see. Mrs. Travers kept trying to include Maggie in the conversation. But Maggie answered all her questions with one-word answers.

Even that was a struggle. The only thing that kept

her going was petting Gus, who had lodged himself under the table, across her feet.

"Maggie, you're awfully quiet tonight," Mrs. Avery said, giving her a searching stare.

"Sorry," Maggie replied, struggling to smile. "I'm just—" She couldn't think of a good excuse.

"She's just worrying about how I'm going to beat her at the meet tomorrow," Andrea boasted, reaching across the table to spear more fries. "No offense, Mr. Avery," she said, "but these fries I made are incredible!"

Everyone laughed. Maggie had never seen Andrea in such a good mood. It was as if the unhappier Maggie got, the happier Andrea became. As if there were only enough happiness in the house for one of them.

Maggie's mother kept sneaking glances at her. Maggie knew what she was thinking. That one appointment with Dr. Marsh wasn't going to be enough.

Mom thinks I'm crazy. Andrea thinks I'm crazy— my boyfriend thinks I'm crazy. The whole world can't be wrong, Maggie decided glumly. Maybe I *am* crazy!

She could barely listen to the conversation.

She kept picturing Miranda, standing so ghostlike, staring at Maggie and Justin from the hedge. And then vanishing into thin air.

She pictured the canopy bed. The beautiful canopy bed that had held such horror for Maggie.

Such horror.

Such horror and—the answer?

Did the bed hold the answer to what this was all about?

Was there more to the dream? Maggie wondered. If I finished the horrible dream—if I saw the face of the attacker as well as Miranda's face—would it clear everything up for me?

I'm tired enough to go to sleep right now, Maggie decided.

I have to get to the end of the dream. I have to put this nightmare behind me.

"I'm going to get some more soda," she lied, getting up from the table.

Everyone was staring at her. Her mom started to her feet with a worried look.

"I'm just going to the refrigerator, Mom," Maggie said. "Chill out."

She smiled at everyone, but she smiled too hard— which only made her feel like a lunatic.

Then she bent down to whisper in her mother's ear. "I've got to go lie down, I'm totally wiped out. Dr. Marsh said I should get some sleep. Cover for me, okay?"

She patted her mom's arm and hurried away.

In the kitchen, she took a long drink of milk straight from the carton. Milk always calmed her down, even cold milk.

She took the stairs two at a time, heading for her bedroom.

I'll go to sleep. I'll dream, she told herself.

And I won't wake up till I know the answer to this mystery.

I won't wake up until the dream is over.

And then maybe—maybe—the whole real-life nightmare will be over too.

Eagerly, Maggie crossed the hall to her bedroom, pushed open the door—

And saw that the canopy bed was gone.

· *chapter*

21

"*H*uh?" Maggie gaped in shock.

Gone. Vanished.

The bed was gone.

In its place stood an ordinary box spring and mattress on a metal frame, made up with Maggie's pink sheets and white afghan.

Still in the doorway to her bedroom, she heard the back door slam. Footsteps up the front stairs.

Andrea appeared in the hallway, a smug expression on her face. "Didn't Mom tell you?" she asked. "Dr. Marsh said she didn't think the bed was good for you, the way you were always obsessing about it."

"But I *need* it!" Maggie cried, feeling herself lose control. She grabbed Andrea's shoulders. "Where is it? What did she do with it?"

She knew the answer even as she asked the question. She stormed past her sister into her room.

Maggie was sure she would find the canopy bed in there.

But there was only Andrea's dumpy old bed, with her raggedy old teddy bear lying on the pillow. Same as always.

"*Where is it?*" Maggie shrieked. "Where's the *bed?* What have you done with it?!"

"I didn't touch your stupid bed," Andrea replied with a sneer. Mom had it moved to the attic. She got one of those moving men over here. And Mr. Avery helped."

The attic?

Maggie knew the house had one, but she'd never been up there.

She pushed past Andrea, hurrying out into the hall. "Where is it?" she demanded.

Andrea pointed up at the ceiling. "I think that's what you're looking for," she said.

Maggie stared up at the ceiling. For the first time, she saw there was a short rope dangling from a metal hook, and a rectangular crack in the ceiling. A trapdoor.

"The stairs pull down," Andrea told her. "But don't even think about going up there. Mom will totally freak out."

"I don't care what she does," Maggie snapped.

"Listen, Maggie," Andrea said. "Mom sent me in to get you to come back. Mrs. Avery made chocolate pie because Mom told her it was your favorite. You've got to come back. Even if it's just for a few minutes."

Maggie leaned back against the wall with a sigh. The bed would have to wait for her.

Andrea tugged on her sister's hand. "Come on, Maggie. Mom is worrying."

All the sugar Mrs. Avery had left out of the lemonade had been added to the pie. It was so sweet, it made Maggie's teeth ache!

But she plastered on her best fake smile and made it through dessert.

Settled in the new bed, Maggie fell asleep the moment she closed her eyes—or that was the way it seemed anyway.

When she opened her eyes again, the room was dark and silent. She squinted at her clock radio. As she watched, the numbers flipped silently forward: 3:21.

She lowered her feet to the floor.

Everyone was asleep, she was sure.

The coast was clear. Maggie could sneak up into the attic, climb into the canopy bed, and try to finish her dream.

Who killed Miranda? Who? she asked herself, tiptoeing to the bedroom door.

Silently she crept out of her room and into the hall, taking it one step at a time, trying to keep the creaking floorboards to a minimum.

It wasn't until she reached the end of the hall that Maggie realized her mistake. Even though she was tall, there was no way she could reach the cord on the trapdoor.

She had to get a chair.

Please, don't anybody wake up! she begged silently.

A few seconds later, she set the chair down carefully and climbed up on it, praying that Gus wouldn't wake up and come sniffing around. A couple of barks from Gus, and her mom and Andrea would be up for sure.

The trapdoor was wide, with a set of wooden stairs that slowly opened downward as she pulled. Even though she pulled it down one inch at a time, the contraption creaked noisily.

Maggie wiped the sweat from her forehead. Every few tugs, she stopped to listen for sounds from her mom's bedroom.

Finally the attic stairs had reached the floor. Bending forward, she started up them, one step—and one creak—at a time.

She climbed up to a tiny space whose walls were the sloping eaves of the roof. The rafters were low, and she had to stoop. The only window was tiny and covered with a thick layer of dust, letting in dim moonlight.

But she could see it clearly—the bed, pushed against the far wall. The canopy was pressed right up against the low ceiling.

Maggie's heart began to pound as she made her way over to it.

Will I be able to sleep? she wondered, gazing at it in the tiny, dark space.

Will I be able to return to the dream?

Will I be able to solve this frightening mystery once and for all?

Maggie stopped a few feet from the bed—and gasped when she saw that someone was sleeping in it.

chapter
22

Maggie moved closer on trembling legs.

The shadows deepened around the bed. The canopy made it even darker.

But Maggie recognized the sleeping girl at once. Miranda!

I'm staring at a ghost! Maggie realized.

She could hear Miranda's shallow breathing.

Maggie moved closer and reached out a hand.

I'm close enough to touch her.

I'm going to touch a ghost. Will I feel anything at all?

Her hand touched Miranda's shoulder. Maggie felt warmth beneath the thin T-shirt.

"Hey—" Miranda jerked up, her eyes wide and angry. She scrambled out of bed.

Maggie let out a startled cry and stumbled back.

Miranda's slender chest heaved as she breathed

hard, glaring through the darkness at Maggie with wild, angry eyes.

She took a step toward Maggie.

Maggie shrank back. But there was nowhere to go. Her back was already pressed up against the low, sloping wall.

"Are you—really a ghost?" Maggie choked out.

Miranda didn't reply. Instead, she bent down and picked up something from the floor beside the bed.

The knife!

The blade glinted in the pale moonlight from the dusty window.

Just like in the dream, Maggie thought.

Miranda raised the knife.

With a desperate groan, Maggie rushed forward. She gripped the girl's arm.

They struggled.

"You—you're real!" Maggie cried. "You're not a ghost!"

Miranda pulled out of Maggie's grasp. Breathing hard, she took a step back.

Maggie frantically searched for an escape route. But Miranda was planted between Maggie and the stairs. There was nowhere to run.

"I—I dreamed about you, Miranda!" Maggie cried.

The girl's eyes widened in surprise.

"I dreamed about you. Every night. In this bed," Maggie continued. "Someone stabbed you. It was so horrible. I—"

The girl laughed, a strange, shrill, mirthless laugh.

"Someone stabbed Miranda," she said. "Poor Miranda."

"Huh?" Maggie gaped at her. "What are you saying? You're not Miranda?"

The girl shook her head. Her long hair swayed around her face.

"But in the dream—" Maggie started.

"Miranda had to die," the girl interrupted. "Miranda was mean—like you!"

"Like me? I—I don't understand," Maggie stammered. "Who killed Miranda? Did you?"

The girl nodded. "Maybe," she said softly, her eyes burning into Maggie's. "Maybe I had to kill Miranda because Miranda was mean."

"But who *are* you?" Maggie demanded.

"Gena," the girl replied. "Wasn't I in the dream?"

"I—I don't know," Maggie told her. She edged toward the attic stairs.

"I'm Miranda's sister," the girl said angrily. "Why wasn't I in the dream?"

"I don't know. Really!" Maggie repeated, swallowing hard. Her throat felt dry as attic dust. "I don't understand the dream, Gena."

"I do," the girl replied sharply. "Miranda always said she had powers. Miranda made you have the dream. Miranda wanted to warn you about me. Miranda is so mean."

Maggie edged a little closer to the steps. "And you killed her, Gena? You stabbed your sister?"

Gena raised the knife. "I had to. I *told* you. Miranda was mean—like you."

"But I'm not mean, Gena. Really!" Maggie cried, seeing the anger in the girl's eyes.

"You want to lock me up again, don't you?" Gena accused. "You want to lock me away in that gray hospital. But you can't, Maggie. You can't! I got out once. I'm not going back!"

"When?" Maggie asked, desperate to keep her talking. "When did you get out?"

"Just before you moved here," Gena said. "I came back to my house. But everyone was gone. So I had to live up here."

"In the attic?"

Gena nodded.

"You've been living up here the whole time?"

Gena nodded again. "Your house is empty all day long. I had the place to myself. I don't eat much, so nobody missed the food I took out of the fridge. And the way you all leave your keys laying around—it was so easy to get one made. I could come and go as I pleased."

Suddenly she sprang forward without warning.

She grabbed Maggie by the hair and pulled hard, with surprising strength.

"Ow! Let go!" Maggie cried out, trying to break free.

But Gena had caught her off balance.

Maggie fell hard.

Grasping Maggie's hair, Gena pulled her head back, exposing Maggie's throat.

She raised the knife.

She held it high as they both heard rapid footsteps up the creaking attic stairs.

"Hey!" Andrea's startled face appeared in the open stairwell.

"Hi, Andrea," Gena said casually as if they were old friends. "I'm going to kill your sister for you now."

chapter

23

Gena tugged Maggie's hair hard until Maggie's head rested on the bed. "I'm ready, Andrea," she announced.

"Andrea!" Maggie cried in horror. "You—you *planned* this with her?"

Andrea climbed into the room. "Wait—" she said softly.

"Do you really hate me that much?" Maggie shrieked.

"Wait!" Andrea insisted, louder, moving toward them over the creaking floorboards. "Who *are* you?" Andrea cried to Gena. "Let *go* of her!"

"But I'm doing it for you, Andrea," Gena replied, sounding hurt. "She's mean to you. She's mean—like Miranda."

"For me?" Andrea cried. "What did you do for me?"

"I did everything for you," Gena replied softly.

"Maggie—I've never seen her before!" Andrea cried. "Never! You've got to believe me!"

"Stop her!" Maggie choked out, staring up at the knife.

Gena pulled harder on her hair, bending her back on the bed. The pain roared down Maggie's body, paralyzing her.

"Stop her, Andrea! Don't let her kill me!" Maggie pleaded.

"I did everything for you, Andrea," Gena continued, ignoring Maggie's terrified cries. "I hurt those two girls for you. So you could be on the swim team."

"You *what?*" Andrea shrieked.

"Oh, no," Maggie gasped. "She's the one who hurt Dawn and Tiffany. I don't believe it."

"And I pushed the knife into your sister's pillow, Andrea," Gena confessed proudly. "You know. To give her a little scare. To get her ready for tonight."

"But I don't *want* you to kill her!" Andrea wailed. "Who *are* you? What is going on? How did you get into our house?"

"Shut up, Andrea," Gena said softly.

She lowered her gaze to Maggie. "It's time," she whispered. "It's time for mean sisters to die."

With a desperate cry, Maggie reached up and grabbed Gena's hand, the hand that gripped her hair.

"Ow!" Gena cried out as Maggie dug her fingernails into the girl's wrist.

Gena jerked her hand free, releasing Maggie's hair.

She brought the knife down—hard and fast.

Maggie rolled out from under it.

The blade cut into the mattress an inch from Maggie's side.

Maggie struggled to pull herself off the bed.

But Gena dove on top of her, knocking her back with such force that Maggie's head bashed into the headboard.

Just like in the dream!

The thought flashed into Maggie's mind.

The nightmare—it's coming true.

They struggled on top of the mattress. Gena was too strong, too determined.

She brought the knife down again.

Maggie uttered a terrified moan as everything went black.

chapter

24

*E*verything went black.

But Maggie realized she was still alive, still struggling in the darkness. The knife had missed her.

She squirmed free from Gena's grasp. Rolled off the bed.

And realized why everything had gone dark.

Andrea had pulled the canopy down on top of them.

"Quick!" Andrea urged. "Maggie—quick!"

Andrea held one end of the canopy and motioned frantically to Maggie.

Maggie didn't hesitate. She grabbed the other end of the canopy—and they lowered it over Gena.

Gena kicked and struggled, trying to get free.

The hand holding the knife shot out.

Andrea grabbed the wrist, and pulled open the fingers. The knife bounced onto the floor.

"Wrap her up!" Maggie cried.

Working together, the two sisters began to wrap the squirming girl in the canopy.

"What on earth—" Mrs. Travers cried from the stairwell.

"Call the police! Hurry, Mom!" Maggie called.

They heard her run to the phone to call the police.

Gena was wrapped tightly in the canopy. She stopped struggling and lay still on the bed.

"I—I hope you can explain this all to me," Andrea said, holding Gena down, struggling to catch her breath.

"I think I can," Maggie replied, forcing a smile. "For the first time, I think I can."

"Do you really think Gena's older sister made me dream that dream? Do you really think she was trying to warn me about Gena?" Maggie asked.

Mrs. Travers sipped her coffee. "That's as good an explanation as any," she replied thoughtfully.

Maggie, Andrea, and their mom were sitting around the kitchen table, sipping coffee from white mugs. The police had just left, taking Gena with them. Through the kitchen window, they could see the red morning sun lifting itself over the trees.

"Old Gus really protected us, didn't he?" Maggie said, rolling her eyes.

Hearing his name, Gus trotted in from the living room. He rested his head on Maggie's thigh.

Maggie patted his warm head. "What a good guard dog, you are, Gussie. Yes. You're a real killer. Thanks for telling us we had someone living with us in the house this whole time!"

Gus gazed up at her adoringly, as if he were being given the highest praise.

Maggie smiled at Andrea. "You saved my life."

Andrea shrugged. "Hey—it was the least I could do."

"You can have the canopy bed now," Maggie offered, grinning.

"No thanks. *You* have it," Andrea replied.

"No, really," Maggie insisted. "You have it."

"No way!" Andrea cried.

"Maybe we'll give it to Gus," Mrs. Travers suggested. "He *deserves* some bad dreams!"

"Could I have a water bed?" Andrea asked their mother suddenly.

"Yeah. You could practice your breaststroke in it!" Maggie teased.

"There's nothing wrong with my breaststroke," Andrea insisted sharply. "It'll be good enough to beat you at the meet!"

"The swim meet!" Maggie cried in alarm. "It's today—and we've been up all night!"

"What a nightmare!" Andrea shrieked.

"Please—" Maggie rested a hand on top of her sister's. "Don't ever use that word in this house again."

"Nightmare! Nightmare! Nightmare!" Andrea chanted.

"Sisters," Mrs. Travers muttered dryly, shaking her head.

Gus nodded his head as if he agreed totally.

"Good night, all," Maggie said, climbing up and starting to her room. "Good night—and sweet dreams."

About the Author

"Where do you get your ideas?"

That's the question that R. L. Stine is asked most often. "I don't know where my ideas come from," he says. "But I do know that I have a lot more scary stories in my mind that I can't wait to write."

So far, he has written nearly three dozen mysteries and thrillers for young people, all of them bestsellers.

Bob grew up in Columbus, Ohio. Today he lives in an apartment near Central Park in New York City with his wife, Jane, and thirteen-year-old son, Matt.

Dear Readers,

Welcome to *Fear Street* — where your worst nightmares live! It's a terrifying place for Shadyside High students — and for YOU!

Did you know that the sun never shines on the old mansions of Fear Street? No birds chirp in the Fear Street woods. And at night, eerie moans and howls ring through the tangled trees.

I've written nearly a hundred Fear Street novels, and I am thrilled that millions of readers have enjoyed all the frights and chills in the books. Wherever I go, kids ask me when I'm going to write a new Fear Street trilogy.

Well, now I have some exciting news. I am writing a brand new Fear Street trilogy right now. The three new books are called **FEAR STREET NIGHTS**. The saga of Simon and Angelica Fear and the unspeakable evil they cast over the teenagers of Shadyside will continue in these new books. Yes, Simon and Angelica Fear are back to bring terror to the teens of Shadyside.

The new **FEAR STREET NIGHTS** will be published Summer 2005. Don't miss it. I'm very excited to return to Fear Street—and I hope you will be there with me for all the good, scary fun!

R L Stine

THE NIGHTMARES NEVER END . . . WHEN YOU VISIT

FEAR STREET®

Next: *DOUBLE DATE*

Girl-chaser Bobby Newkirk boasts to his friends that he can go out with both identical Wade twins, Bree and Samantha, in one weekend. But Bobby soon discovers that dating quiet Bree and wild Samantha may prove fatal. He's sure one of the Wade twins is out to get him—the question is, which one?

FEAR STREET® —

WHERE YOUR WORST NIGHTMARES LIVE

ALL-NIGHT PARTY

THE CONFESSION

THE PERFECT DATE

KILLER'S KISS

THE RICH GIRL

THE STEPSISTER

By bestselling author

R.L. STINE

Simon Pulse
Published by Simon & Schuster
FEAR STREET is a registered trademark of Parachute Press, Inc.

feel the fear.

FEAR STREET® NIGHTS

A brand-new Fear Street trilogy by the master of horror

R.L. STINE

In Stores Now

Simon Pulse
Published by Simon & Schuster
Fear Street is a registered trademark of Parachute Press, Inc.